Appalachian Christmas Stories

A gift to

_____

from

_____

_____ , 19___

Illustrated by

Jim Marsh

Appalachian
Christmas Stories

Compiled and Edited by
James M. Gifford
Owen B. Nance
Patricia A. Hall

The Jesse Stuart Foundation
Ashland, Kentucky
1997

Appalachian
Christmas Stories

Copyright ©1997

FIRST EDITION

Library of Congress Cataloging-in-Publication Data
Appalachian Christmas stories / compiled and edited by James M. Gifford, Owen B. Nance, Patricia A. Hall.
    p.   cm.
    ISBN 0-945084-63-3
    1. Christmas--Appalachian Region, Southern--Literary collections.
2. Appalachian Region, Southern--Social life and customs.
3. American literature--Appalachian Region, Southern.   I. Gifford, James M. II. Nance, Owen B. , 1971- .   III. Hall, Patricia A. , 1945-   .
PS554.A67 1997
810.8' 0334--dc21   97-11221
                                                  CIP

Published by:
The Jesse Stuart Foundation
P.O. Box 391
Ashland, KY 41114

Contents

There is a special place in heaven for the people
who take in unwanted children

Dedicated to Clara Moore Clark

Clara M. Clark, with grandsons
Daniel C. Gifford (infant) and James M. Gifford
c. 1947

Preface

The Christmas season calls forth many memories. In this book, stories, essays, and poems weave a garland of the Christmas experience of the mountain people of Southern Appalachia. All of us at the Jesse Stuart Foundation hope that each of you who reads this book will find in these pages the love for others that energizes the true spirit of Christmas.

Many friends of the Stuart Foundation have contributed to this modest volume. Thomas D. Clark granted us permission to use a chapter from his book *Pills, Petticoats, and Plows: The Southern Country Store.* Loyal Jones and James Goode submitted stories that combine well with material from the literary estates of Jesse Stuart and Billy C. Clark, both managed by the Jesse Stuart Foundation. Anne Caudill suggested that we include Harry Caudill's "Christmas Comes to Lord Calvert," and the University Press of Kentucky kindly gave permission to reprint this piece, which appears in Caudill's book *The Mountain, The Miner, and The Lord and Other Tales from a Country Law Office.* Mary Ellen Miller provided a Christmas poem by her late husband, Jim Wayne Miller, and Marlin W. Blaine, a retired employee of Ashland Inc., contributed two delightful Appalachian versions of "The Night Before Christmas."

My office staff--Patricia A. Hall, Owen B. Nance, Yvonne Melvin, and Bridget C. Tolliver--helped at every stage of production. Jim Marsh designed the cover and created the illustrations. Pamela Wise and Associates, Inc. produced the camera-ready pages.

My grandmother Clara Moore Clark (1892-1978), who raised me, would have enjoyed the stories in this book. She could have retired before the 1957-58 school year, but she chose to teach another year so that I could be in her room in the eighth grade. One of my shining memories of that year was her daily reading. Every day, after lunch, we were required to put our heads down on our desks (at the time I thought that was so that we could rest) and she read to us in serial fashion from Jesse Stuart books and stories. It was 1958, and I remember it as vividly as if it happened yesterday. I couldn't wait for the next day's installment. I found two role models that year, and I set myself on a course to become a teacher. Later I realized that my interest in the history and literature of Appalachia began with my grandmother's readings and also her personal stories of teaching in a one-room school.

When I was a small child trying to grasp the story of Christmas, I imagined that my grandmother was a lot like Jesus--she knew how to love and she knew how to forgive and she lovingly sacrificed herself for others. Whatever good I have done in this world and whatever good I may yet accomplish is a tribute to Clara M. Clark, a great teacher and a splendid role model. In loving devotion to her memory, I dedicate this book to her.

James M. Gifford

Santa's Visit

Jesse Stuart

"But you told me Santa Claus would come tonight," Glenna said as she followed her mother from the stove to the kitchen table. "You told me if I'd be good Santa Claus would come tonight and bring me a doll. You said he'd bring me candy!"

Mom didn't answer Glenna. She lifted the pan of hot, steaming cornbread from the oven. Then she cut it into squares with a case knife. She lifted each square from the pan with a spatula and put it on the bread plate.

"Tell me why Santa Claus isn't coming," Glenna asked Mom.

"I've told you once," Mom said. "Go to the window and look at the snow on the ground. Santa Claus is snowbound. The snow is too deep for his reindeer and his sleigh!"

"But, Mom, you told me that Santa Claus went to the housetops with his reindeer and his sleigh!" Glenna said. "If he can drive them to the housetops, it looks like he could drive them through the deep snow and bring presents and toys to all the good boys and girls!"

Mom didn't know what to say. Glenna wasn't yet five years old. And she had been as good as she knew how to be through October, November, and December. Mom had told her that Christmas would soon come and if she wanted fruits, candies, and toys she would have to eat her food at the table. She couldn't go outside into the frosty air without her mittens on. She couldn't say naughty things to her playmates, or be selfish with her brother when they played together with only a few toys. When Glenna disobeyed, Mom would remind her that Santa Claus would know the little boys and girls that had been naughty when Christmas came. Then Glenna would be nice, for she desperately wanted Santa Claus to visit her. So when Mom told her she thought Santa Claus would be snowbound, it was hard for Glenna to accept. She was disappointed.

"But Mom, I want Santa Claus to come," Glenna said, hanging to Mom's dress and crying.

"Glenna, didn't Mom tell you Santa Claus would be snowbound?" Sophia said.

Sophia was my oldest sister, and she understood

that Santa Claus was snowbound. She was 12 and I was 10 years old. She understood about Mom, too. Sophia knew why Santa Claus hadn't been able to get to our shack. The heavy snow, 22 inches deep, that had fallen two weeks before in Beecher's Cove was still on the ground. Sophia and I knew that the time wasn't far when we'd have another little brother or sister. Mom didn't walk much in the snow. She certainly couldn't walk 5 miles over the mountain to Greenwood. She'd have a mountain to go down, and the paths might be slick. When she came back home to Beecher's Cove, she'd have a mountain to climb.

There was another reason why Santa Claus might miss our shack this year. Pa was down sick. He'd had influenza and gotten up too soon and had suffered a relapse. We had barely enough money to buy food. That is why Sophia and I never expected Santa to visit us. But James and Glenna expected him to drive his reindeer over the snow, even if it was 22 inches deep where it wasn't drifted, and many feet deep in some of the drifts. They expected him to come down the chimney with a bag of toys and fill their stockings.

"Come to supper, children," Mom said as she put the plates of hot cornbread on the table.

When we gathered around the table with its scantily-filled dishes of hot food, Mom fixed a few slices of buttered hot cornbread for Pa. And she took him a small pitcher of cold buttermilk. When she returned from the front room where Pa had lain from the time the heavy snow had fallen, she found us eating our suppers. Mom sat down and there was a worried look on her face. There were dark circles under her eyes. She hadn't any more than sat down when Glenna began asking her if she thought Santa Claus would get through the drifts and bring candy, fruits, and toys to her and James. Then Glenna told Mom how good she had been, and that she knew Santa Claus wouldn't forget a good little girl.

Tears came into Mom's eyes and ran over the dark half-moon circles and down her cheeks.

"I wonder if Mary, the Mother of Jesus, ever worked harder than I have," Mom said. "I wonder, sometimes, if she ever had more worries! It's awful when you want to do something and can't!"

"Don't worry, Mom," Sophia said. "If Santa Claus doesn't get here this year, maybe he'll be able to come next year. Maybe there won't be any deep snow next year. Then he won't have any trouble getting to our house!"

"But I want him to come THIS year," James said. "I don't want to wait another year! That's too long to wait!"

"Maybe he'll come tonight," Mom said half-heartedly.

"I'll hang up my stocking," James said.

James and Glenna were then so eager for Santa Claus to come, and so excited about what they thought he might bring them, they could hardly eat their suppers.

"Now you must eat your food," Mom told them. "Remember, if Santa Claus is able to get here at all, he'll be here tonight."

Just as soon as they had finished supper they wanted to go to bed. They wanted to go to sleep and wake up the next morning with something in their stockings and shoes. When they pulled off their shoes, they set them near the fireplace where Santa Claus couldn't miss them when he came down the chimney. When they pulled off their stockings, Sophia took down the fire tongs from a nail, and hung Glenna's stocking there. On the other side of the fireplace, she took down the pothooks and hung James's stocking on this nail.

"Now your stockings are hung by the chimney with care," Sophia said. "Let us hope that Saint Nick'll find 'em! Let us hope that he'll be here!"

That was assurance enough for James and Glenna. Sophia put Glenna in her bed and James in my bed. On these cold winter nights, after the big fire died down in the fireplace, the house got COLD! Sophia slept with Glenna, and I slept with James so we could keep them covered and warm. Mom slept in the room with Pa so she could wait on him throughout the night.

"This will be a bleak Christmas for us," Mom said as soon as Sophia came back into the kitchen. "They expect Santa Claus. I'm afraid he won't be here! If we only had something!"

Sophia didn't say anything, and I didn't say anything. We sat in silence, watching the fire. Suddenly there was a loud knocking at the door.

"Wonder who that could be?" Mom said. "Shan, open the door."

When I opened the door, a gust of cold wind blew past an old man who was standing there before me shaking like a white oak leaf in the winter wind. He had a bundle of clothes across his shoulder, tied to the end of a stick. He didn't have gloves on his hands.

"Son, could a man find shelter for the night here?" he asked me.

I could hear his teeth chattering above the cracking of the wood on the fire. "I can feel that big fire you have, plumb out here," he said as I looked at Mom for an answer.

"Your father is sick, Shan," Mom said. "You are the man of the house!"

"But, Mom," I said. "I don't know what to do!"

I was thinking of the beds. We didn't have a bed for him, unless he slept with James and me. But I couldn't say that to him.

"You know that your Pa and me never turned

anybody out in our lives," Mom said. "And never on a night like this!"

"Then come in, Mister," I said. "Come in and share our fire!"

The old man shot past me like a bullet. He got up so close to the fire that smoke came from his pants. And lumps of ice and snow melted from the strings and straps on his boots and ran into a little stream across the rough stone hearth into the ashes. When the icicles melted in his gray mustache and the gray beard on his face, he wiped the water away with a big, soiled, red bandanna with one hand, while with his other hand he held his turkey of clothes. Mom and Sophia watched the big man as he gathered warmth from the fire.

"You'd better watch yourself," Mom said. "You'll get too hot. After you've been so cold, it will not be good for you!"

"I know, Ma'am," the old man said, "but I might nigh froze to death! And if I'd a-been turned down here, I would have froze. I wouldn't have tried to go on!"

Mom went into the kitchen while the stranger stood before the fire. She brought a wash pan filled with ice water.

"Sit down now, Mister," she said. "Take off your boots and put your feet in this water. If you don't, I'm afraid your feet will frostbite!"

The man did as Mom told him. He pulled off his weather-scarred boots and his socks that were filled with holes. He put his feet into the water. Then he put his hands down beside his feet. His hands were big and gnarled, like the ground roots that spread from an ancient tree. He had hands like Grandpa's hands; and Grandpa was a timber cutter. Melted snow water still ran from his mustache and beard. And he groaned with pain as he kept his hands and feet in the cold water.

"I'm afraid you've frost bitten your hands and feet," Mom said. "And this is the best remedy I know!"

"It is that, Ma'am," the old man said. "I've done it many a time when I used to come home from the timber woods! This remedy will stop frostbite. How kind of you to think of it! I was too cold to think!"

"How far have you walked?" Mom asked.

"About thirty miles today," he said.

"Thirty miles in weather like this?" Mom said.

"Yes," he said. "Before I got here, I stopped at seven homes! And, mind you, Ma'am," he grunted as he sat bent over in his chair with his hands and feet still in the pan of cold water, "they were good looking homes. And each one had a Christmas tree, and there was warmth and brightness within. And people were laughing and talking, and they were happy. And when each door opened I could smell the food and feel the warmth, and it made me sick down deep within."

"You've not had your supper?" Mom asked.

"No, Ma'am, I've not," he grunted.

"Then you shall have something to eat," Mom said. "Shan, put a fire in the stove."

"Oh, how kind of you, Ma'am," the old man said.

I went back into the kitchen and built a fire in the stove. When I came back into the front room, the old man had his hands and feet out of the pan of water and was putting his boots on. The icicles had melted from his beard and mustache, and the bright, warm fire had dried them. There was a good color in his face where it wasn't covered with long, white beard. His lips were no longer as blue as the skin of a wild grape.

"Ma'am, this is the nearest I've ever come to freezing to death," he said as soon as he had tied the last buckskin boot string. "Now, I'll tell you who I am, and what I'm doing. Sorry I was too cold to tell you awhile ago!"

He got up from his chair. He was so tall his head almost hit the joists of our low front room. "My name is Rufus Isom," he said. "I'm from Bruin Creek in Ellit County. I've been on the road two days. I thought I could walk to my son John Isom's place for Christmas Eve. He lives on Hood's Creek in this county. Do you know where that is?"

"You've got 20 miles to go yet!" I said.

"I've always been able to walk 40 miles a day," Mr. Isom said. "But I've only made about 30 miles a day through this snow!"

"My name is Martha Powderjay," Mom said. "And this is Shan and Sophia. I have two more, Glenna and James, in bed asleep, waiting for Santa Claus to come. Mick Powderjay my husband, is bedfast from a relapse of influenza. He's been bedfast for a month and a half!"

"Mrs. Powderjay," Rufus Isom said, "it's hard for me to believe that so many people living in big houses, and with so much, turned me from their doors. And you, under these circumstances, have taken me in and given me the warmth of your fire, saved my feet and hands from frostbite. And now you are going to feed me!"

Mom and Sophia went into the kitchen and I sat before the fire with Rufus Isom.

While we sat before the fire, I noticed that he looked at the empty stockings hanging up on each side of the fireplace. Then he looked around at our furniture. He put his boots near the fire and warmed his feet through his boots. He warmed his big gnarled hands. His giant body absorbed warmth before our fire until his face was flushed and his eyes looked sleepy.

"This fire is wonderful," he said. "Who made it?"

"I did, sir," I said. "I made the fire and got the wood!"

"Mighty good for a boy your age," he said.

I didn't have long to talk with Rufus Isom before Mom came to the door and called him to the kitchen for supper. She had baked a pan of hot cornbread. She had a pitcher of milk, a dish of potatoes, fried tender pork loins, meat gravy, and coffee. That was more than we'd had for our suppers. Mom gave him the best we had. Rufus Isom ate like he was starved.

After he had eaten his supper, Sophia stacked the dishes, and Mom and I went back to the front room with Rufus Isom.

"Will Santa Claus come tonight to the little fellers?" he asked Mom.

"I'm afraid he won't, Mr. Isom," Mom said. "I had to tell them before they went to bed that Santa Claus was snowbound. I couldn't lie to them. I didn't want them to get up in the morning expecting something and be disappointed!"

Rufus Isom looked into the fireplace. And he was very silent. Then he looked at the empty stockings. His big blue eyes moved in their wrinkled sockets as he looked first at the fire, then at the empty stockings, and then he would glance over and look at Mom. Mom looked into the blazing fire thoughtfully. Maybe she was thinking of other Christmases when the stockings that hung before our fireplace had been filled with candy, nuts, and fruit, and there were toys for each of us stuffed in our shoes, or lying behind them, or hanging from a Christmas tree. But this Christmas was different. It was the only bleak Christmas I could remember. We had always loved Christmas time. We had waited from one Christmas to the next in joyful expectancy.

"Mrs. Powderjay, would you care if I take a few things from my turkey and put into your little ones' stockings?" Rufus Isom asked Mom. "I started to take them to my son John's two little ones. But I won't get there in time. It will be late tomorrow before I get to his home, with 20 miles yet to go!"

"But you have brought them for your own grand-children!" Mom said.

"Just some little things," he said. "Santa Claus will come to my grandchildren anyway, and I'll make some more toys for them after I get there. Now I want to do something," he talked on softly, "to make Christmas happier for you and your children, since you have done so much for me! You have saved my life! Every place I stopped, I was told to come to the Powderjays. They told me that you people would keep wayfarers for the night!"

"We never turned anybody from our door," Mom said.

Then Rufus Isom opened his turkey and brought

out a sack of stick candy. The sticks were yellow, red, and white. It was peppermint candy. He divided the candy and put an equal number of sticks in each stocking. Then he took a small package of hickory nuts and hazelnuts from his turkey. He divided the nuts and put an equal portion in each stocking.

"I've got some little things here I made," he said. "See, it's hard for us to get toys back where I live. We make most of our toys!"

He had made little rabbits and squirrels from acorns. He put a little set of acorn cups and saucers into Glenna's stocking, and he put the rabbits and squirrels in James's stocking. He had whittled out little baskets from hickory nuts and walnuts, and he divided them between the stockings. He put a cornstock fiddle and bow and an elderberry squirt gun into James's stocking. He put a little churn, dasher, and lid, that he had made from a hollow sourwood, into Glenna's stocking.

"Just some little things that I sit around before the fire and make nowadays," he said. "Just make them to kill time. Tonight it does my heart good that I brought them!"

"Those things are beautiful," Mom said. "You are a real Santa Claus!"

Sophia and I looked on eagerly as he hung the stockings back on the nails. And a smile came over

Mom's face. She was pleased. I'd never seen her look happier. Santa Claus would not be snowbound now! Santa Claus had waded through the snow without his reindeer and sleigh. He had walked 60 miles, too. He'd been two days on the road. And Santa Claus was nearly frozen, and he was mighty hungry when he came to our shack.

But he had come, and it would be a happy Christmas!

That night Rufus Isom took half of James's and my bed. But James was asleep. And I didn't care. Rufus Isom was so big that it took half the width of the bed for his broad shoulders, for he slept on his back. And he was so long that his feet stuck over the bed. James and I slept on our half the bed, or a little less than half the bed, that night. And once in the night James talked in his sleep about Santa Claus.

Long before daylight, I was awakened by the crowing roosters. I got up and built a fire.

While Mom and Sophia were getting breakfast, I fed the livestock, hogs, and chickens, and I milked the cow. When I returned to the house, Rufus was up and dressed. He was sitting before the fire, when something happened. Glenna and James woke at about the same time, and they ran to the fireplace to look at their stockings.

"Santa Claus HAS come!" Glenna shouted. "My

stocking is full!"

"Look at my stocking!" James shouted as he followed Glenna.

A big smile came over Rufus Isom's face as he watched Glenna and James, who passed by him, too excited to see him. When they found the nuts and the long sticks of peppermint candy, they shouted with joy. When they found the little toys, they were so happy they could hardly speak. They ran in the kitchen to show Mom and Sophia.

"Santa Claus wasn't snowbound," Glenna shouted as she went through the door toward the kitchen. "He wasn't snowbound, Mom! He got here!"

"It wasn't too cold for Santa Claus, Mom," James shouted as he followed Glenna.

"No, James, Santa Claus is here now," Mom laughed. "It was too cold for him to go on last night. He slept with you and Shan!"

"Oh, where is he, Mom?" James asked.

"Where is Santa Claus, Mom?" Glenna shouted.

"He's sittin' before the fire in the livin' room," Mom said.

Then James and Glenna ran from the kitchen to the living room, screaming with joy as they raced to be the first one to see Santa Claus.

James jumped on his lap. Glenna ran behind his chair and put her arms around his neck.

"Santa Claus, I love you," she said. "And I'm glad you weren't snowbound after all!"

"Oh, thank you, thank you," Santa said. "Now I must be on my way," he said as he took the basket of food Mom was holding for him.

James and Glenna began to cry.

"If I come back to you next year," he said, "you'll have to dry your tears. I must go now to see the good little boys and girls I didn't get to see last night."

At last the time came for Santa to say good-bye to all of us. With a basket on his arm, and a turkey of toys, clothes, and candy fastened to the end of a stick that rested across his shoulder, he was on his way.

We stood at the window watching him walk down the little path toward the deep white valley. The icy wind tried to pull the long white beard from his face. Once Santa Claus stopped and looked back. He saw our faces against the windowpanes. He waved to us and we waved to him. Then we watched him walk down the deep, white valley, until he was out of sight.

Appalachian Christmas Angel

James B. Goode

Mrs. Idaho Missouri Patterson had been the last one on Christmas Eve. Baby number twelve had been easy. He, more or less, only had to "catch" it when it emerged into the back bedroom of the little coal camp shack.

The first one that morning had been Lark Barnes whose foot had been crushed in a rock fall at the C Seam mine on Looney Ridge. He had been reluctant to visit Lark after the incident at the hospital. The whole thing had been an accident. Picking coal out of a crushed foot is a tedious procedure and he didn't mean to grab Lark's toe bone. The last thing he remembered was Lark's red face as he rose to his feet and hit him between the eyes with his very large right fist. He was awakened after nurse Judd broke a vial of ammonia under his nostrils and fanned him with a surgical towel.

But Lark had been cordial and apologetic. He had

said that his fist had gotten ahead of his thinking and that was why he had knocked him out. But everybody knew that Andrew Larkin Barnes had a bad temper.

The rest of the day had been hectic for Doc. Several children had come down with Chicken Pox, one high school girl had contracted infectious Hepatitis, and one boy had fallen from a grapevine swing and stoved himself up pretty badly–there were no broken bones, just cuts, scratches, and wounded pride. Several pregnant women had needed his special attention–their complaining, moaning and groaning had about pushed his bachelor patience to its limit. He had written prescriptions for everything from codeine cough syrup to nerve pills. It was ten o'clock at night Christmas Eve and he was bone, dead tired.

Dr. Dupree drove his old Model-A through a heavy snow to the company hotel on the hill next to the school house. He stopped by the fountain and got a vanilla coke and trudged up to room 211 to collapse on the sofa and listen to the radio while he finished the coke.

When he got up to get in bed, he didn't even bother to take off his pants and shirt. Almost as soon as he dropped his brogan shoes on the wooden floor, he was asleep–snoring like a hog in a corn field.

He dreamt there was a plague in the coal camp and he was the only physician. Hundreds cried out for his help. Thousands died, waiting for him to come to their aid as he ran, waist deep, in a pool of cold molasses. The place looked like a Civil War battlefield. He had entered a tiny, board and batten shack on Hunky Street and was administering to a very ill, feverish little girl when he heard someone knocking at the door. He was busy giving an injection in the tiny, white hip. At first he ignored the knock. But the knocking continued. It was a steady, persistent rapping on the door facing

He awakened in an instant, sat up in bed, and tried to focus in the dark room. He could see a tiny stream of light through the crack at the bottom of the door. The knock was coming from the door. There was a slender shadow which moved back and forth in the light of the crack.

He swung his tired feet over the side of the bed and stabbed at his shoes on the dark floor. He managed to get half his feet in his shoes and straighten his twisted shirt and pants while groping for the door knob.

The door stuck for an instant and then flew out suddenly. He caught it just before it hit a little girl who stood shivering in the hallway. Tears streamed down her tiny cheeks and she sobbed every other breath. She wore a gray wool coat soaked with snow and muddy patent leather shoes. Her blonde curls hung in wet rivulets on her shoulders.

"You have to come with me nnnnnnnow," she stammered. Her chin quivered from some deep emotion which had overwhelmed her mind. Big tears threatened to spill over her eyelids and rush down like a spring flood.

Doc Dupree was still attempting to adjust to the light and the shock from the door opening so quickly on such a sad scene.

"Come in little girl and let me get you a dry towel." He reached for her tiny hand.

"I don't have ttttime to," she said. "My mmmamma is very sick and needs your help," she withdrew her hand and hid it in her coat pocket.

"What's wrong with your mamma?" Doc asked hurriedly.

"We think she's got a bad fffflu. That's why I come to get you. She is burning up with fever and she won't eat nnnnothing. She's been sssseein' things that ain't there!" She removed her hand from the coat pocket and reached for his.

"Where is she?" Doc asked.

"We live in Proctor in Devil's Holler." She tugged at his shirt tail.

"Honey, that's 15 miles from here and it snowing like a bat out of hell out there," he exclaimed.

She ignored his pessimism. "I rode our old mule,

Dragon, over here. I ffffigured we could take your car back and it would be twice as fast." She smeared a dirty streak across her chin with the back of her hand.

"All right," he said. "You have to give me a chance to tie my shoes, get my bag, and find my overcoat."

He quickly threw additional medicines and his new stethoscope into the worn black leather bag he carried on house calls. He struggled to get on his old wool coat. The lining was loose in one arm and his big hands hung on the slick material. Finally, he backed his hand out, pushed it forward again, and the arm slid into the sleeve.

They walked briskly down the long hotel hallway. The little girl stumbled on the gaps in the rubber runner as they sped toward the stairwell. When they reached the Model-A he couldn't help but laugh when he saw that the little girl had tied old Dragon to the front bumper.

Doc untied the grass rope. "Let's put him in this utility shed until we can come back after him," he suggested.

They pulled some frozen grass from beside the shed, threw it into a corner, and led Dragon into the tiny interior. Doc quickly shut the door and replaced the bent nail in the hasp.

He'll be fine until we get back," he reassured the little girl.

The Model-A was stubborn to start, but it finally hit and began to purr like a contented kitten. Doc opened the passenger's door, picked up the little girl, and placed her on the bench seat. He ran around to the driver's side, jumped onto the seat, slammed the door, and started off down the graveled road leading to Proctor.

When they had passed the last house in Looney Ridge, it occurred to him that he didn't know the girl's name.

"I bet such a pretty girl has a pretty name," he inquired.

"My name is Faith Simpkins," she hung her head between the collar on her coat and blushed.

"That's a beautiful name," Doc replied. "I don't particularly like mine," he said. "Mother named me after my grandfathers on both sides. Hector Lum Dupree just doesn't fit." He toyed with the name emphasizing the LUM in the middle of it. "Hector LUM Dupree–then HECTOR Lum Dupree–then Hector Lum DUPREE." None of them seemed to work for him.

The little girl fell silent. She had quit sobbing and the tears were dried in dirty streaks on her face. By the time they reached the halfway point at Wise Gap, she slept with her head leaned against the door jam. Doc concentrated on the snowy dirt road–peering through the smear left by the stubborn vacuum windshield wipers of the Model-A.

Doc began to think about how he arrived in Looney. He had graduated from the state university medical school and the coal company had practically recruited him right off the graduation platform. Dean Newberry had known the superintendent and arranged for an interview six months before graduation. The superintendent had attended the graduation ceremony and presented him with a letter stating the "Board of Directors of Looney Creek Coal Company have unanimously agreed to employ Hector Lum Dupree upon his graduation from Medical School at the University of Kentucky as a general practitioner at the Looney Valley Company Hospital."

Doc's idea of where he would practice medicine and where he actually did were as different as a redheaded stepchild in a family of blondes. He had often imagined himself in a starched white jacket with "Dr. Dupree" embroidered on the pocket gliding down a freshly polished tiled hallway in some far away hospital in Chicago or Pittsburgh. Looney Valley Company Hospital was far from that apparition. The tiny wooden hallway, which divided the six in-patient rooms, was a far cry from what he had seen in his dreams.

Looney Creek Coal Company did pay him a retainer and he was able to collect a five dollar doctor's fee when he made a house call. He made a living–barely. When he did treat people outside the coal camp, he most often was paid with a sack of meal, a chicken, or a gallon of molasses.

He shook the little girl awake as they approached the outskirts of Proctor.

"Where did you say this holler was?" he asked.

She rubbed her sleepy eyes and pointed to a tall pine tree they were approaching on the right side of the car.

"Turn here!" She said quickly. "This is it!!!"

He turned the narrow wheels of the Model-A onto a tiny dirt road which followed the crooked creek up the hollow. A pack of mongrel dogs ran beside the car, growling and snapping at the wooden spokes on the wheels. Faith rolled down the window and yelled, "Now Charger, quit that! You go on home and I'll give you some smoked bacon when we get there." The red bone hound ran ahead of the car, swinging his hips from side to side–running as if he were somehow off-balance.

The board and batten house they approached at the head of the hollow was not unlike many that Doc had seen in the mountains surrounding the coal camps. The unpainted exterior had weathered to a silver gray and the windows sagged until some of them were setting at crazy angles. A porch ran across most of the front and there were a few pine boughs tied in ropes along the banister. Doc could see the lights from a tiny Christmas tree through the window. There was a small Hemlock wreath on the door which contained a picture of Jesus, apparently cut from a magazine, in the center of the circle.

Doc took a brief look at the picture while Faith yanked at the rawhide string for the drop latch on the door. Jesus was in the garden–he looked peaceful as he prayed. He didn't look like the tortured face of the crucified Jesus Doc had seen in the colored pictures at the center of his King James Bible.

Faith flung the door open and revealed a very modest living room which had, as its centerpiece, a Warm Morning coal stove which sat on a metal stove board. A few straight-backed bark bottomed chairs were scattered about the room. There were a few pictures, possibly of relatives, and a big oval print of Jesus and the Disciples in the upper room taking communion. Jesus was leaned to one side and he held a silver chalice in an upraised hand.

"Momma's in the back bedroom–hurry." Faith let out a big sigh. "I've got to run and tell Momma's sister, Aunt Sudie, you're here. Sudie's real old and couldn't come help Momma. I'll be back faster than you can shake a stick!"

Before Doc could say anything she disappeared

out the door and was swallowed by the cold night and the blowing snow.

Doc moved quickly to open the door to the bedroom. Faith's mother lay in an old iron bed in the right corner of the room. A pink chenille bedspread was pulled up around her chin. Her teeth chattered and the whole bed shook from her convulsions.

"Mrs. Simpkins, I'm Doc Dupree from up at the Looney Camp. I'm here to help you!" Doc opened his black bag and removed the stethoscope.

"Thank the Lord, you mmmmmade it." She was chilling and her chattering barely allowed her to speak. She attempted to rise from the bed and hold her hand out to Doc. He grasped the hand and gently lowered her back onto the wet sheets.

"Looks like your fever is breaking," he said. "That's a good sign. I'm going to listen with this scope, so you just take some deep breaths and let them out slowly."

Doc gave her a sheet to cover her front and carefully pulled down the back of her old house dress. Mrs. Simpkins labored as she tried to take deep breaths. Her lungs sounded raspy. She wheezed when she let out the air. Doc moved the stethoscope around her back, listening intently. Finally, he dropped the scope to his neck and said, "Mrs. Simpkins, I believe you have double pneumonia. Now, I'm not going to kid with you–this is dangerous and you have to mind everything I say. You can't be exposed to anymore cold air. I want complete bed rest for you–I don't even want you to get up to go to the bathroom. I'm going to give you a dose of antibiotics now and you'll need to take one of these every four hours until they are all gone. You can't miss–not even one."

Mrs. Simpkins coughed. Deep from within her lungs the air gurgled from the mucous created by the infection. She pulled the bedspread back up around her ears.

"Praise the Lord from whom all blessings flow!" She managed to say in a very weak voice.

Doc glanced to the bedside table which held a worn Bible, a dim burning kerosene lamp, and a picture of Faith.

"You have a brave little girl, who has a lot of grit Mrs. Simpkins. It took a lot of courage for a girl that young to ride a mule fifteen miles in a snow storm to bring me to your bedside. She must love you very much." Doc patted her on the forehead.

Mrs. Simpkins looked bewildered and then a big, dark cloud passed over her face. "My Faith has been dead for two years now. She passed over from the flu on Christmas day." Tears began to trickle down her flushed cheeks.

Doc was speechless. His heart began to pound and flutter. "The little girl in the picture–is that Faith?"

he gently asked.

"That's my onliest baby–she's one of the little angels in heaven now." Mrs. Simpkin's face suddenly became peaceful and her tear stained chin began to quiver. "The onliest things I have left of hers is this picture and her little wool coat hanging in that closet."

Doc went over to the closet and pulled back the flowered cloth covering the doorway. There, in the center of the closet, was the gray coat Faith had been wearing when she knocked on his hotel door in the Looney Ridge coal camp.

Joey's Best Christmas
Loyal Jones

Joey always loved Christmas, but one Christmas was both scary and wonderful. When he was seven, Joey's school Christmas party was on the afternoon of Christmas Eve. Afterward he walked up the farm lane to his house and called for Ranger, his Redbone hound. He whistled as loud as he could, but Ranger did not come.

"I'll bet he's off chasing rabbits," Joey said to himself.

He went into his house, calling for his mother or father, but no one was home. Then he saw a note on the table. It read, "We have gone Christmas shopping. We'll be home before suppertime. Love, Mom."

Joey changed his clothes. He had an idea. His father and mother never had a Christmas tree. Instead they put holly and mistletoe in the windows and over the fireplace. That was the way their own parents had celebrated Christmas. Joey's idea was that he would go cut a Christmas tree like the one at school. He would pop corn and make strings of it to decorate the tree. He would surprise his parents. He changed to jeans and a sweater. He put on his boots, coat, and gloves.

In the woodshed he found the saw his father used for sawing firewood. He looked around and whistled for Ranger. Ranger was still gone. Joey went across the hill behind his house. He remembered where there were pretty pine trees just a mile away. He walked across another hill and up a hollow between hills. He then climbed across a steep hill. It had gotten colder. The clouds were darker and lower, and a cold wind began to blow. He'd better hurry, he thought. It might snow. He liked the idea of snow for Christmas.

Soon he saw the pine forest. He looked around for the prettiest tree. There was one out in the open with perfect branches. It was taller than Joey. A snowflake touched his face. He looked up. More flakes were coming down, and the wind was getting stronger. He thought he had better cut the tree and start home.

He lay on his side under the pretty tree, took the saw and began cutting. It was harder than he thought, but the yellow sawdust was as bright as if the sun were shining on it. Soon the tree fell, and he looked at it proudly. By now the snow was coming down fast. He heard the wind whistling in the tall trees.

He took his saw in his left hand. He hooked his right arm though the lower branches of his Christmas tree and started toward home. A sudden gust of wind sent snow and sleet into his face. His cheeks burned. The wind sounded like an angry cat in the trees. The snow came thicker. He could see only a few feet in front of him, and he was not sure just which way to go. He tried to make out the hill he had come over, but the snow was too thick for him to see it. He wished Ranger were here. He'd know the way home.

He stopped to think. How many hills had he come over? He remembered three. He started walking in the direction he thought was toward home. He tried to recognize trees. Nothing was familiar. The snow had covered the trees and the ground. All was white. The wind drove the snow in gusts. It was getting dark. For the first time he was frightened.

He walked on. He was cold now. His cheeks were red from the wind and snow. His fingers were numb. He came to a huge tree, and he leaned against it to rest for a minute. He saw that it was hollow on one side. There was room for him inside. He left his Christmas tree and saw and went inside. It looked like a little shed. He could no longer feel the wind. He took off his gloves and put his hands inside his coat. They began to get warm. He jumped up and down to warm his feet. He soon felt better and sat down to rest. He was scared though.

He tried to think what he should do. He knew he was lost. He must have gone in the wrong direction. He had never seen this tree before. He wished again for Ranger. Dogs always know the way home.

It was quite dark now. He was pretty warm and could probably stay the night in the hollow tree. But it was Christmas Eve. He wished he had never thought of the Christmas tree. The holly and mistletoe would have been enough. He wanted to be home. Maybe it would stop snowing and he could see the way. Maybe his father would come looking for him. But no one would know that he had come into the woods. How could they find him?

He searched through his pockets and found a piece of hard candy and a cough drop. He ate them. He jumped up and down again until he was warm. He was suddenly tired and sat down again. The wind still howled, and the snow came down. He fell asleep.

He slept for a long time. Then he felt something cold on his face and woke with a jump. It was Ranger's cold nose that he felt. Ranger was glad to see him and licked his face. Joey was so happy to see Ranger that he hugged him.

"How did you find me?" he asked the bounding dog. Then he remembered that dogs could follow a person's tracks by their scent.

"Can you find the way home, Old Ranger," he asked. Ranger bounded out of the tree and started off, barking over his shoulder at him.

Joey dug in the snow for his father's saw and took hold of his Christmas tree. It was heavy with snow. He shook it and it became lighter. He started after Ranger. They went over a hill with Ranger barking every few steps. He followed happily, dragging his tree. The snow had stopped coming down.

Soon he heard voices. He stopped to listen, but Ranger ran ahead, out of sight. He feared he was leaving him behind. Soon he came back, whining and urging him to hurry.

"Joey, Joey," he heard his father's voice.

"Here I am, with Ranger," he called back.

Soon he saw a lantern ahead and his father was before him, standing tall behind the light.

"Oh, Daddy, am I glad to see you!" he cried.

"No gladder than I am to see you," his father said and swung him up in his arms. Then his father yelled over his shoulder, "Here he is. I've got him."

He heard someone answer. Soon his three tall uncles were there. They whacked him on the back and asked him how he was. Ranger frisked and jumped.

"I was cutting us a Christmas tree," he said, "and I got lost in the snow, but Ranger found me." The tall men all patted Ranger, and the dog looked proud.

Joey's father started up the hill toward home.

"Wait," Joey said. "I have to get my Christmas tree." He ran back to his tree. His father took it from him, and one of the uncles took the saw. They started back, with Joey walking happily among them, holding to his father's hand. Their shadows leaped against the white trees and bushes from the light of the lanterns.

They walked down the hollow and over the last hill beween them and their house. As they reached the top, one of the uncles shouted, "Look there." They all looked up, and there was a single star in the sky where the clouds had parted. The woods were lighter now, all white everywhere. Joey looked toward home and saw lights in the windows.

His father began to sing: "There's a song in the air. There's a star in the sky. There's a mother's deep prayer and a baby's low cry. And the star rains its fire while the beautiful sing, for the manger of Bethlehem cradles a king."

It was the only verse his father remembered from a song he had learned in school when he was a little boy. It was beautiful to Joey.

They came down the hill shouting and laughing, for they were happy to bring Joey home. His mother and aunts came onto the back porch, and his father shouted, "We have Joey. He went to cut a Christmas tree. Ranger found him."

Joey's mother ran to meet them and hugged him so tightly he couldn't breathe. All of his aunts hugged him too. He was embarrassed, but he was proud to have such a loving family.

Nobody scolded Joey because they were so glad to have him back home. His mother and his aunts went to cook supper. An uncle made a stand for the tree, and his father brought it in. They put it in a corner. His mother and his aunts came from the kitchen, and they said it was pretty.

"We'll pop corn after supper and decorate it," his mother said.

They all ate together, and he told them about his trip for the Christmas tree. Joey's mother gave Ranger leftover food and patted his huge head. She even gave him a piece of pie. She hugged Joey several times. His uncles all mussed his hair and looked at him fondly.

After supper, when the dishes were washed and dried, they all sat by the fireplace, and his mother popped corn. Joey's aunts got needles and long threads and made strings of popcorn. They all decorated the tree together. It was the prettiest tree Joey had ever seen. His mother brought in a box of presents and put them under the tree. They were all shapes and colors.

After a while Joey got sleepy. His aunts and uncles said goodnight and left. Joey went upstairs to his bedroom to put on his pajamas. His father and mother came and sat on either side of his bed.

"We're glad you are back home and safe," his father said. "But next time we'll go with you to get a Christmas tree."

"We love you very much," said his mother. "We'll have a good Christmas tomorrow."

They turned out the light and left Joey to his thoughts. He could see the snow on the tree outside his window in the dim starlight. Ranger came upstairs on his soft feet and put his head on Joey's pillow. Joey patted his smooth, broad head.

"Thank you, Ranger," he said, and the dog lay down beside his bed. Joey felt drowsy, and so he said his prayers. He thought of his Christmas tree with the presents underneath. He knew that tomorrow was going to be the best Christmas he would ever have.

Christmas on the River
Billy C. Clark

Winter had come to the river banks. The air was cool and sharp, and the rivers were beautiful. There were thin layers of ice along the edges of the rivers, and the leaves that had missed the current had been captured by the ice, and the meager sun shone and turned the leaves many colors. Now and then a brown ball would fall from a giant sycamore tree and break through the ice and the water would bubble out and run in small streams across the surface.

One day as I was sitting on the river bank, I heard a group of boys coming through the willows. Christmas was only a few days off. At the church, the boys said, sacks of hard candy would be given to all the young people. Anyone who wanted a sack could have it. All you had to do was to walk inside the church and get it.

As I watched the splinters of river ice, I thought

only of the tall sacks of hard rock candy they had talked about. To them the candy might not have meant much, but to me it was something that cost more than I ever hoped to earn.

During the next few days, all I thought about was the sack of candy. I watched the rivers, silent now and with little current. I thought of walking inside the church and getting my sack of candy and as quickly as possible hurrying back inside the willow grove and working my way to the creek. Of course people inside the church would stare. But if I was fast on my feet, they wouldn't have long to stare.

As Christmas day came nearer, I began to sneak to the top of the bank and measure with my eyes the distance from the giant maple to the door of the church. And the more I measured the distance, the farther it seemed to be. While I was inside the church I would not have the time to stop after I had picked up my sack of candy to thank God for it. But then, I could do this easy enough when I reached the banks of the river again. Maybe, when I grew up and earned enough money to buy good clothes and have my hair cut, I could go back inside the church and thank Him proper.

Christmas day came at last to the valley. I was more scared than I had ever been in my life, more scared than the day the *Gordon C. Green* had slipped past, as I swam across the Ohio River.

At the mouth of Catlettscreek, I stopped and bent over the small stream and splashed the cold water against my face, and the wind dried it and cold pimples ran up and down my back. As I thought of walking inside the church, the bumps grew larger than the wind could make them.

I hurried to the mouth of the Big Sandy and waited at the top of the bank behind the maple until I was sure that everyone was inside the church. I closed my eyes a moment and then ran out from behind the maple and didn't stop till I was at the door of the church. I stood for a minute to catch my breath and maneuvered around in front of the door as carefully as I would have moved around a snapper turtle.

The door opened with a squeak and I sneaked inside. At the far end of the room a woman stood beside a large wooden table. On top of the table were white sacks. The woman at the table called out the name of a class and a group of girls stood and walked single file down the aisle. As they passed by the table, they were each handed a sack. Then another name was called, and a group of boys even smaller than myself passed by the table, reaching for the sacks of candy that seemed so big that they weighed the boys down.

As I stood at the front end of the room, I became more scared than ever. All I could see were the tall sacks of candy. Right now I was too scared to move, yet I had come much too far to turn back. I scanned the room for the boys that I had seen at the river. I waited until they stood and started down the aisle, and then I fell in behind them like a duck that belongs to the same flock. I kept my eyes peeled to the floor, never once looking up. The legs of the table came into sight and I raised my head and stared into the eyes of the woman at the table.

"This boy is not in my class," she said, in a voice that seemed to shake the walls of the church.

"Nor mine either," another woman answered from the first bench.

"Nor mine," another voice said.

"He doesn't belong here at all."

Tears filled my eyes, and for a minute I was too scared to move. People were staring at me and many of them shaking their heads. I knew now that all I wanted was to make it back to the rivers. This red brick church was not for me. I realized that I had been planning on getting something that did not belong to me. I turned and ran as fast as I could, down the steps of the church, and I didn't stop even at the small creek. I splashed in and the water circled my knees, and on the other side I fell to the sand and buried my head in my arms and cried. A short time ago, the sack of candy had meant almost as much to me as the two rivers.

Now it meant nothing. Even if I had gotten it, I couldn't have taken it home. They would have thought that I had stolen it–or begged it, which would have been worse.

I stayed on the banks of the river below the house until the shadows crossed the water. Tears had frozen on my face and where I had waded the creek my legs were so cold they were numb. Then I heard footsteps on the frozen grass. And when I looked up Mom was standing over me. She did not quarrel because I had stayed away from home so long without her knowing where I was. She knelt beside me and I felt her arms around my shoulders.

"Hush now," she said. "Times come that even a man has to tell what's wrong. Tell me."

And stuttering worse than a jay bird I told her how I had wanted to steal the sack of candy, expecting her to break a willow switch at any moment.

But there were tears in her eyes too. And she held me close.

"Maybe it is better for our kind to give our thanks under the willows here. Prayers have far enough to climb without being hemmed in by the wall and the roof of an old building."

"But," I said, "maybe God don't know that I'm down here. He didn't see me in the church, and I didn't see Him."

"Hush now with foolish talk," Mom said. "If He can see a little bird like a sparrow, you know that He can see a big boy like you."

Mom pulled a handkerchief from her pocket and wet it over her tongue and wiped my face and the wind dried it.

And that evening Mom left the house and did not come back until after dark. I heard her come in during the night and pull the covers over us as she always did. But she stayed by our bed longer than usual this time. And the next morning when I woke I felt something hard under my pillow and when I reached down to find out what it was, I pulled out a small sack. And inside the sack was hard rock candy.

I jumped from the bed and ran into the room where Mom and Dad slept. "Look, Mom!" I yelled. "Look what God has given us!"

"Pon my word," Mom said, "who'd have thought a prayer could have traveled that fast? Now, if you want to make the Lord happy, you'll share with the rest of the family."

As I walked out of the room, I wondered why my brothers and sisters didn't ask the Lord for a sack of candy themselves. I sneaked a handful out of the sack and stuck it into my pocket, so that they wouldn't know how much the Lord had given me. I divided the rest with them and then I ran to the river bank to eat what was in my pocket.

When I reached the bank, I was so happy that I wanted to run and shout to both rivers. I looked into the clouds and thought of my prayer scaling the blue walls faster than a stream of smoke. But as I ran through the trees, I slipped over a stump and fell to the earth. The hard rock candy fell out of my pocket and rolled over the sand, picking up sand like a snowball scooping up snow. One by one the pieces rolled down the steep bank and into the river. The Lord had seen me sneak the candy into my pocket back at the house.

Mom was right: He didn't have any trouble at all seeing me here on earth.

A Little Bit of Santa Claus

Thomas D. Clark

Once each year the southern country store took on a delightfully new appearance and a fresh, exciting aroma. New boxes, bales, barrels, and sacks obstructed the passageways and overflowed onto the shelves and counters. This seasonal addition of new stock was even permitted to break into the holy circle about the stove. A general assortment of holiday goods was superimposed over and around the regular stock. Barrels and boxes of candy were rolled in between the sugar, coffee, meal, and flour or put down on the counter tops among the thread and knife cases. Bags of coconuts were ripped open and the tops of the sacks rolled down displaying their fuzzy brown wares awaiting purchase by the cake makers. Boxes of oranges were opened and leaned end-up against the counters. Barrels of apples were distributed among the nail kegs and benches about the stove circle. Toys were suspended from the ceiling among the lanterns, water buckets, horse collars, buggy whips, and lard cans, or they were mixed in with the everyday merchandise of the glass cases. On top of the counters were small wooden boxes lined with red paper and filled with sawdust and shavings, and the contents were ruffled into a seductive state of confusion. These contained the firecrackers, torpedoes, and Roman candles.

Above the commonplace everyday odors of the stores there was a change. There was a much stronger overtone of cheese. Oranges and apples gave a richness; burned powder from fireworks added an acrid flavor, and above all of this was the fragrant bouquet of Bourbon or the raw tang of corn whisky. Newly opened tubs of corned mackerel sat well back out of range of careless tobacco chewers. Here was an assortment of merchandise and rich smells which made indelible impressions on several generations of Southerners and which are to many, even yet, a reminder of Christmas. Clarence Nixon wrote of his father's store in his understanding book, *Possum Trot*, "We stocked up with fruit in December, and I still think of Christmas when I smell oranges in the country."

The South was a land of deep sentimentality. Family ties were close, and the hard years following the war tended to knit them even more securely. Christmas was a time of family rededication and a season of erasing old and irritating scars of discord. It was a period for visiting and feasting. Celebration of the holiday was the one institution which came through the war unchanged except for the matter of simplification. Until 1915 rural observance was uncontaminated by commercialization. Simple gifts were passed around, and these, as a matter of course, came from the country store.

Much of the masculine taste in celebration ran to boisterous forms of expression. For more than fifty years the liquor barrel furnished ample cheer for all customers who could rake together enough cash or "stretch" their credit to buy a quart of Kentucky or Maryland Bourbon, or a half-gallon of North Carolina corn. A quart of whisky was admittedly a vigorous start toward a glorious Christmas season. For the temperate, however, a package of firecrackers was enough holiday amusement. One little nickel package of Chinese firecrackers provided plenty of Christmas joking and pranking. A favorite stunt was to explode the tiny cylinders at the heel of some humorless deacon, with the hope of starting him into "cussing." Another was setting them off near a pair of mules in a storehouse yard. The number of runaways made many a good celebrant regret that there was such a thing as Christmas. But there was the more pleasant aspect to this form of amusement.

Thousands of country children were happier waking up in a cold farmhouse on Christmas morning because Santa Claus had not forgotten the firecrackers and Roman candles.

There were also torpedoes which exploded with thunderous repercussions when dashed on the floor underneath girls' feet, and Roman candles gave great gusto to the Christmas celebration. They lifted the holiday spirit high into the air in sputtering balls of varicolored fire followed by sulfurous tails which outdid Halley's comet in the eyes of backwoods cotton farmers. Sometimes they were used in sham battles which generally wound up unhappily. But all in all, there was something in the violent cracking of fireworks that gave zest to Christmas week, and which marked the completion of one crop year and the beginning of another.

Unlike their Yankee brethren, Southerners saved their fireworks for Christmas instead of the Fourth of July. There seems to be little fundamental reason for this traditional difference between the sections. Some have explained that because the siege of Vicksburg was ended on the Fourth of July, Southerners refused to celebrate the day in any other way than that of going to fish fries and political picnics. This is hardly true. Perhaps the weather conditions were a more vital factor, but whatever the reason, the stores did not stock firecrackers for the July trade. It has always seemed that for a Southerner to shoot firecrackers and Roman candles in the summertime was just about as incongruous as killing hogs in August.

The louder the noise the country-store customers could make, the happier they were. When the last firecracker fizzled out, the more adventuresome resorted to the use of black powder and anvils for noise making. Powder was packed tightly into the round and square holes of one anvil, and a second one was placed securely on top of the charge so that when the powder was ignited both anvils rang out in loud metallic tones which could be heard for miles around. Traditionally, anvil shooting was a part of every Christmas affair. Country stores, school and church grounds boomed with thunderous impacts of these black-powder charges, and evidence of this primitive custom has lingered in many farmyards. Few of the half drunken celebrants who fired their steely blasts realized that they would dehorn their anvils in the explosion, and many a "muley-headed" block of steel was carried home to tell its mute tale for years to come of a hilarious country Christmas.

All of the stores kept black powder during the years 1865 to 1900. One entry after another is for the inseparable combination of powder, shot, caps, and sheets of wadding, and it is a remarkable fact that with all of the storekeeper's harum-scarum methods of keeping stock there is no record of powder kegs exploding. Yet many powder barrels and kegs were left as carelessly exposed inside store buildings as were barrels of sugar and coffee.

The Winchester Arms Company along with all the other manufacturers of guns and ammunition were quick to shift manufacturing practices after 1865 to that of supplying ready prepared ammunition which could be used in the new-type breech-loading guns. But the muzzleloader remained popular in the South for forty years after Appomattox. The typical reluctant rural southern attitude toward a change in plow tools and implements prevailed toward guns. A muzzleloader would shoot, and a man could hit birds, rabbits, and squirrels with it; it took time to load, but time was cheap. Because of this unprogressive attitude, the powder, shot, and cap trade remained constant in the stores. Not only did merchants sell supplies for ammunition, but they made some profit from the sale of detachable tubes which were screwed into the base of powder chambers and on which percussion caps were exploded. Literally thousands of entries were made in account books for these outmoded hunting supplies. The muzzleloading gun was an institution, and if not an entirely safe and certain one, at least most people had learned its weak points. They were slow to accept new and improved arms which involved such a fundamental change as that of loading pre-pared ammunition into the breech.

When at last the primitive weapon of the antebellum South was outmoded, orders for shot and powder were changed to demands for boxes of shells, and the South quickly became a land of the single-barrel breech-loading shotgun. Remington, Stevens, Winchester, Iver-Johnson, L. C. Smith, Sears, Roebuck, and Montgomery and Ward distributed thousands of these cheap weapons throughout the South. Rabbit hunters much preferred the light choke-bore, single-barrel twelve- and sixteen-gauge guns. When they were loaded with their characteristic yellow hulls charged with three drams of black powder and one and one-eighth ounces of number-six shot, they became bush cutters and rabbit killers of a high order.

By December crops were gathered, and it was safe to set the woods and fields afire. For a whole week during the Christmas season hillbilly and cane-cutter rabbits lived in misery. Christmas Day was the big day of this season of hunting. Sedge fields and heavily wooded bottom lands rang out with the constant firing of hard-kicking breechloaders. Scarcely a southern community got through the season without some type of casualty. Occasionally accidents were slight; sometimes they were the result of an irresponsible prankster's forgetting that shot and powder were wholly devoid of a sense of humor. There were, however, unhappy tragedies which caused many southern families to bemoan Christmas Day for many years. Persons were killed or maimed with unhappy regularity in the big hunting sprees. Livestock was killed and fences and buildings destroyed. Yet these big hunting parties were as characteristic of the holiday season as were coconut cakes, apples, oranges, and raisins.

Of a more doubtful virtue was the considerable country store trade in pistols. These instruments of rowdy community life were seldom if ever displayed in the stores in open cases, but they could be had either by immediate private purchase or on special order. Cartridges, however, were always openly available. Southerners of all races desired to make big noises and sporting impressions. They bought pistols which they shot at random into the open air, and sometimes they emptied them without discrimination into both enemies and friends with the same deadly results. There was a spirit of rowdiness and irresponsibility which was handed down from the frontier antebellum South to the younger Southerners of the postwar period. Young men had a love for lethal weapons. Knife cases in country stores had their share of constant admirers flocking around and gazing at the long bladed wares, and almost always knives were adjudged on the basis of their length of blade and potential powers of destruction. This respect and admiration for knives was carried over to a fondness for guns. Perhaps not all of this attitude was of southern origin. At the time when postwar stores were being organized and the general business scale was upward, colorful stories of life on the Great Plains were finding their way back across the Mississippi River to the South, and doubtless these stories of quick-shooting had much to do with keeping alive the love for pistols. It was a day when many make-believe southern Billy-the-Kids with sharp-pointed handlebar mustaches posed for formal photographs with a brace of pistols across their vest fronts. Certainly, in general appearance, they were fierce men. Along with the unhappy influence of the Great Plains, the excitement of courting, Christmas, crap shooting, and liquor, all seemed to encourage "gun toting." Notes in private papers of merchants and items listed in wholesalers' lists are indicative of this popular gun trade.

Generally pistols sold through the country stores or listed in the "silent drummers" were exceedingly poor weapons. There was the popular Harrington and Richardson "double acting, full nickel plated, rubber stocked" model which sold in the nineties at wholesale for $2.98. This gun fired a standard short thirty-two-caliber bullet sidewise. Competing with it was the well-known Iver Johnson "owl head" which was a double-acting piece of unreliable rubber-stocked artillery. Perhaps this gun was found on more people in the South when they were arrested for one sort of public disturbance or another than all other types of hip-pocket guns put together. There was a third popular brand of "short artillery" which was sold extensively throughout the cotton states. This was the cheap, short-barreled pistol called the American Bulldog, which was bought in dozen lots for the individual unit whole sale price of $1.25.

Seldom was there a public Christmas entertainment in the rural South at which there were no altercations and where cheap country-store pistols did not play an insidious part. Under the laws of all of the states it was illegal to carry concealed weapons, but these laws were universally ignored. In fact, in the whole irregular pistol trade there was an excellent commentary of general regional attitude toward laws and community conduct.

Southern backwoodsmen galloped home from their best girls' houses at Christmas firing pistols with wild abandon. So common was this practice in some southern communities that the erratic firing of a pistol by a single man was a sure sign of two things: He had either broken up with his girl, or he was going to get married right away.

Firecrackers, guns, and ammunition were only a small part of the country stores' Christmas trade. During the period of reconstruction, buying holiday goods because of inflated prices was actually a matter of expending a considerable amount of money without getting a satisfactory return in goods. For the first time, rural stores were introducing items which were to characterize the yuletide season in the rural South for the next three-quarters of a century. E. F. Nunn and Company of Shuqulak, Mississippi, sold oranges at a dollar a dozen, apples at sixty cents, dolls at twenty cents apiece, and whisky at two dollars a gallon. E. F. Nunn, the bachelor proprietor, charged to his account the purchase of skyrockets, two candy trunks, four kisses, five candy rolls, one bunch of torpedoes, three packages of firecrackers, three dozen eggs, three pounds of candy, two Jew's harps, and two rattlers. In this benevolent merchant's Santa Claus account was nearly the whole story of the more temperate southern Christmas. Self-explanatory were the eggs and whisky. Even the most temperate Southerner could be prevailed upon to break over and sip a little eggnog at Christmas time. At Raymond, Mississippi, a solvent countryman in 1869 bought of the newly established house of Drane and Dupree a bottle of perfume, a photographic album, a pound of candy, two pounds of nuts, half a dozen oranges, a dozen nutmegs, a bottle of lemon extract, a toy wagon, four dozen apples, a gallon of whisky, six bananas, a toy drum, one Roman candle, and a coconut. Here were all the ingredients except two for a joyous southern Christmas. Missing were firecrackers, shot and powder.

Twenty years later another rural Mississippian at Blackhawk was buying a dozen apples, four dozen eggs, two pounds of mackerel, a box of salmon, seven pounds of cheese, fifteen pounds of onions, a toy work box, four pounds of nuts, six dozen oysters, a box of raisins, and a dime's worth of nutmegs. About the same time merchants in Alabama were stocking oranges, raisins, nuts, oyster crackers, mincemeat, premium chocolates, citron, currants, sardines, toys, glassware, picture albums, coconuts, and bananas.

Fruits and nuts were items of real luxury for the Southerner, and they were purchased only in the spending orgies of Christmas time. Oranges and apples in the extreme southern states were rarities, yet they were both produced on the periphery of the region. Oranges at some time or other became an inseparable part of the general history of Christmas, and especially was this true in the South. By the seventies the account books showed that oranges were bought generally, but it is doubtful that many people knew anything about the history of their production. They, perhaps, believed that oranges could be bought only at Christmas time because merchants never displayed them at any other season.

Families bought a dozen oranges and felt that they were well supplied. Children waked up on Christmas morning to find a golden ball in each stocking, and to discover that Santa Claus, in a generous mood, had left an additional half-dozen by the fireside. Although for the most part anything which went into a stocking was, by a type of domestic common law, the individual property of the child receiving it, oranges were an exception. These were common property and were eaten by the family, in many instances, one at a time. Mothers usually stripped off the peeling and passed the fruit around in segments. Every part of the orange was saved. Peelings were carefully preserved to be used throughout the year as flavoring for cakes, custards, and puddings.

Apples, in the extreme southern states, were as rare in December as were oranges. Crossroads merchants bought them from distributors in Maryland, Virginia, Pennsylvania, and sometimes North Carolina. They were bought by the barrel and were retailed by the dozen, and seldom did the wholesale and retail prices bear any relationship. A barrel of apples cost from three to six dollars, and they retailed by the dozen at from twenty to sixty cents. In many merchants' papers the letters of Henry Wright of Aberdeen, Maryland, appear in the November and December files. He advertised himself as "giving special attention to the southern trade." Certainly he was an important dealer, and his garrulous patronizing letters are long stories within themselves of this aspect of Christmas in the country stores. He well understood that buying apples was for many customers a bit of sentimental extravagance. As with oranges, few members of some families had ever been so profligate as to eat a whole apple at a time. Occasionally pitiful entries in individual accounts show that a dozen apples was the lone recognition which many impoverished customers of country stores could give to Christmas.

Nuts, raisins, and striped peppermint stick candy were common items listed in a great majority of the December accounts. Raisins had a special appeal, and many a farm child pulled brown bunches of these delicacies out of his stocking with more excitement than he showed for new toys. Love for stick candy and nuts came through the war unchanged. Stores bought candy by the barrel and sold it pound by pound at a very good profit. By the end of the century when the days of McKinley prosperity had changed somewhat the financial situation of the country, confectioners began placing a varied assortment of fancy piece candy on the country-store market which sold at a higher price and for a fancier profit.

There were many other Christmas purchases mixed in with the standard entries. Coconuts formed a vital part of Christmas cooking. A ten-cent coconut placed a distinct emphasis upon Christmas feasting. In fact, next to fresh oysters, it gave real distinction to the Christmas dinner. Mrs. M. H. Jennings ordered six coconuts, two boxes of gelatin, and a bottle of lemon extract from an Alabama merchant. She was preparing a rich Christmas dinner for a houseful of company. Six coconuts were sufficient to make enough cakes to last all of Christmas week and well into the new year. Mrs. Jennings' generous order was an example of much of the southern attitude toward food. If one coconut cake was good, then six would be that much better.

Opening coconuts was a real adventure for rural southerners. First there was the sport of punching in the soft eyes in order to drain off the richly flavored milk which was a much better drink than spring water. Then there was the business of cracking the hull and extracting the crust of meat. Often great care was taken not to smash the hull into bits when sawing open the nuts. The lower half of the shell made an excellent bowl for a dipper, and many families of limited resources went through the year drinking water from a dipper made by mounting half of a coconut shell on the end of a strong wooden handle.

Long hours were spent rubbing hunks of the meat

of coconut over coarse homemade graters. The results, however, were nearly always satisfying. It was with a spirit of genuine triumph that southern women placed before their families thick rich coconut cakes. This was almost sufficient achievement to make a full Christmas celebration within itself. There were rivals of the huge cakes which were heavily frosted with the meat of the coconut. Frequent orders for citron, currants, and other types of dried fruits and spices indicated the extent to which fruitcakes were considered a part of every holiday meal.

Along with foods that were bought at the stores or prepared at home was the game brought in during Christmas week. Birds, squirrels, and rabbits suffered tremendous casualties when every man and boy in the neighborhood turned hunter for ten days. Rabbit meat became commonplace, and great platters of bird and squirrel went begging after the first few days. Before World War I, Southerners failed to appreciate with any degree of intelligence their sinful extravagance. Rabbits and birds were thrown away because no one cared to eat them. Shooting a gun was an exciting sport, but shooting it aimlessly at an inanimate target was a senseless waste of money. With the smoke of their valuable woodlands in their eyes, Southerners exterminated game and rich natural resources at the same stroke. Yet the pleasantness of all memories for many generations of rural Southerners were the exciting Christmas hunts and the taste of fresh-killed wild meat.

Southerners generally liked oysters, both canned and fresh, and many of the store books contain records of numerous purchases of this highly perishable food. It is a matter of amazement that a store so thoroughly isolated as was Ike Jones' at Blackhawk, Mississippi, could get oysters through the New Orleans market and keep them fresh for several days. Every box of freight which reached this place had to be hauled many miles over muddy roads on a wagon, yet Christmas always found a stock of oysters on hand. Where transportation facilities were poor and the sale of perishable merchandise was an impossibility, merchants relied upon salt herring and mackerel for a change of diet at Christmas. It was a genuine treat for most families to get a kit of mackerel to sandwich in between salt meat, rabbit, and quail. Cheese enjoyed a position of favoritism on the list of standard yuletide purchases. Where cash resources were limited, one- and two-pound orders were common, but customers who wound up the crop year by breaking even or with a little clear money were satisfied with nothing short of a hoop of cheese. So popular was cheese that even Santa Claus sometimes left wedges of it by hearth sides or crammed into wide-mouthed stockings. He even carried his whim of practicality to a greater extreme and left salt mackerel and coconuts along with meager offerings of firecrackers and fruit. This was the simplest way for a man without funds to ease himself out of an unhappy predicament with his family and keep up the spirit of Christmas.

The Christmas trade was not alone a matter of doing a profitable business in fancy groceries, toys, and gifts, but it was also a matter of buying a large variety of farm produce. Womenfolk saved eggs for weeks to provide funds for holiday shopping. Sometimes frugal customers started in September packing down thirty or forty dozen eggs in cottonseed awaiting the seasonal rise in price. Among the Christmas orders are notes which tell in their simple eloquent way a sorrowful story of poverty. A South Carolina mother scribbled on a rough fragment of scratch paper, "Willie, I send 5 dozen eggs give just what you can and Sammie will trade it out in something for the children times are so hard that is all I want to give them for Christmas."

A strange assortment of produce found its way to the feed rooms during November and December of each year. There were sweet potatoes, butter molded in all designs and in numerous stages of preservation, tallow, home-cured meat, shelled corn, cottonseed, dried herbs, mink, 'possum, skunk, and coon skins, kindling, black walnuts, cowhides, and peanuts. Everything that would bring a little extra cash and could be spared was hauled away to be sold for Christmas money. Crossties and cordwood for gin furnaces supplied a meager income, and many a wagon loaded with crossties was ragged over almost impassable roads by a pair of ill-fed mules to stores along the railroads. The last of cotton and tobacco crops was sold, and ramshackle farm wagons jolted home with their precious boxes, bags, and cans of merchandise. Children listened for the clucking of these wagons over the rough roads, and they rushed out to climb aboard as soon as they came in sight. It was with adroitness indeed that many of the drivers were able to keep their Santa Claus supplies safely out of sight when their vehicles were boarded by a band of expectant children.

Closely associated with the celebration of Christmas in southern farmhouses were the community Christmas trees and parties. These were given primarily for courting couples, but they afforded equally as much pleasure for children and older people. School yards and church grounds were crowded with buggies, wagons, and saddle horses while, inside, half-drunken community wits, dressed in flimsy red suits and shabby cotton whiskers, carried on a stream of humorous banter as they handed down presents from bespangled holly and cedar trees.

Gifts off a country Christmas tree were curiosities indeed. A favorite present for girls was plush-bound photograph albums and memory books. Sentimental females loved these cheap artistic atrocities, and they filled them with family photographs, bits of hair, stray pieces of cloth, pressed leaves, poetic clippings from newspapers and magazines, and personal notes. For the merchants these items yielded a good profit, and many times generous orders for them appeared in the invoices.

Merchants also stocked special assortments of fancy china and glass bric-a-brac to lend color and grace to the useless whatnots and shelves which lined parlor walls. Plates with fancy fruit and floral designs, bowls with berries, fruits, and vegetables burned into them were good sellers. So were the long platters adorned with sad-eyed bass which gave a lasting impression that every hot piece of meat lying on their backs was burning their very souls out. There were platters with luscious halves of watermelons, clusters of rich purple grapes, or bunches of small game. Those with rabbits suspended from a wall made an appetizing scene indeed; it was truly stimulating to a ravenous Southerner to be able to scoop up spoonfuls of gravy from the furry backs of lithographed rabbits firmly glazed in the bottom of meat dishes.

From the end of the war, lamps had a continuous

patronage. There were the tiny little brass lamps with stubborn round wicks which had a constant habit of sticking in the ratchets and refusing to go either up or down. Then there were those of a later period which stood on heavy glass and metal pedestals. These used the improved flat wicks and boasted safety air tubes permitting kerosene to flow freely upward without danger of exploding the glass bowls. But these were commonplace household utensils and were never regarded as things of art. It was not until the era of heavy chandeliers with their gaudy trappings and curlicues which hung in pretentious homes in the cities that colored lamps became a part of the rural merchants' stock. This was an era when church lamps were heavy and ornate monstrosities hanging from sturdy beams at the ends of bronzed log chains. Big-bellied tinted lamps became necessary fixtures all over the South. They were at once indicative of a certain amount of dignity and social well-being. There was always considerable room for doubting that their lighting functions were adequate, but just standing by in their very stuffiness upon center tables they performed a mute service of art. This service actually was that of epitomizing the lowest ebb of a degenerating Victorian taste in the nineties for a South which was trying hard to keep abreast of the vulgar artistic fads of the rest of the country.

Even the "silent drummer" descriptions of parlor lamps were staid bits of formalized commercial prose. One model that bulged voluptuously in exactly the same places and proportions as well-fed matrons of the day was described by the wholesaler as "a Parisian shaped body parlor lamp with a ten inch globe, tinted and shaded in fine enamel finish, beautiful hand-painted flowers, best center draft burner, solid brass oil fount, gold plated foot, twenty inches high to top of globe." These Parisian beauties sold, packed three in a barrel, for $8.29. There were others which had less gold on their feet, and less bulge in their bellies and bosoms which could be retailed for not more than two dollars.

Country merchants stocked fancy cups bearing the highly imaginative legends, "A Present," "Lucky Dogs," "Baby," "Father," "A Souvenir," and "Think of Me." There were quart-sized mustache cups with their built-in china retaining walls. These were adorned with lurid sprays of flowers or lodge emblems and saucy legends designed for the dominating male of the age. The china dashers fought back the unruly ends of handle-bar mustaches from the coffee and helped partly to dispense with the indelicate business of sucking one's whiskers, or having them drip coffee on false shirt fronts.

Companion pieces to the rotund mustache cups

were the big-bellied shaving mugs with their heavy, round, looping handles, and cavernous mouths opening through their side with as much grace as gaping sensuous lips. They, more than mustache cups, symbolized the sternness of manhood in the nineties. Potters were little influenced by the gaudy art of their day in the manufacture of these mugs. Their primary concern was that of making a receptacle which would hold a cake of soap with reasonable firmness while an irate male dragged his whiskers off with a dull straight razor.

Of a distinctly feminine nature were the delicately tinted, flower-decked toilet sets which were composed of from three to six pieces. These contained toilet bottles with globe stoppers, comb and brush trays, manicure trays, hairpin boxes, and powder-puff boxes. They were customary gifts for sweethearts and were sold for one to six dollars a set. Scarcely a rural parlor dresser went without these milk-glass or colored-glass adornments, and nearly always they were displayed as signs of a girl's popularity rather than as necessary fixtures of her dressing table.

A long list of cut and molded glassware was sold to the Christmas trade. Most common of all the vases were the glass flower holders and vases called Bohemian and alabaster. They were delicately colored, but were trimmed in gaudy fins and flounces, which, like pompon lamps, gave them the appearance of a female who had on entirely too many petticoats. There were butter dishes with quaint glass covers, glass hats, slippers, compotes, pickle dishes, and large, round-cut glass berry bowls. These pieces were sold by the barrelful, and scarcely a household, including the humblest cabin, was without some of them. Most practical of all was the covered butter dish which helped in a day of patent fly-minders and peachtree limb-shakers to insure some degree of momentary sanitation for the huge cakes of hand-molded butter.

Standard among the utilitarian sets were the water pitchers and glasses. By accident these were made in attractive designs. Even today along modern southern highways, myriad antique shops are reselling hundreds of pieces of this once cheap country-store Christmas glassware. Along with Bohemian and alabaster toilet sets and vases and the big mugs and mustache cups, the bulging, ugly old floral lamps have found their way to the antique stands. Cheap water pitchers which once sold for as little as a dollar a dozen now bring twice that much apiece. Colored-glass hats, or "toothpick" stands, sold for twenty-eight cents a dozen, and were retailed at ten cents apiece. Now some of them sell for the original price of a gross.

Santa Claus not only brought cheer to the juvenile country South, but he was likewise an agent of cultural taste. In a lefthanded way he was in at the kill of Victorianism on the store shelves, although it was not so gruesome a murder after all. For three generations rural Southerners have found their tenderest memories to be of the crossroads stores and their completely disorganized stocks of Christmas goods. Sentimentality for Christmas historically spilled over into affection for the stores themselves. For the countryman the store at Christmas time was literally a meeting place of stark everyday reality with a fantastic world of temporary but pleasant escape.

Christmas Comes to Lord Calvert
Harry M. Caudill

CLEON K. CALVERT was a man of strong opinions forthrightly expressed. He was also a fine lawyer with a commanding courtroom presence and much eloquence. He practiced his profession in the Kentucky hills for fifty years and was well known in the courthouses of at least a dozen counties.

He was sometimes referred to as "Lord Calvert," a friendly nickname applied by other lawyers because of the costly brand of whiskey he was reputed to imbibe. Once when he was serving as special judge of the Harlan Circuit Court he partook too freely, a fact that became apparent to spectators in the courtroom. When court was called to order the next morning the judge humbly apologized for his miscreant conduct, found himself guilty thereof, imposed a fine as punishment, and paid the money to the clerk.

For many years Calvert was an attorney for Ford

Motor Company. When Ford began buying huge tracts of coal in Harlan, Leslie, and Letcher counties, he supervised the tedious task of abstracting the titles. After this work was completed he maintained a general practice until his death in 1970. He was one of those richly colorful personalities whose extreme individualism once brought renown to the Central Appalachians.

In 1955 I was involved in a lawsuit for title to a tract of coal land. Calvert was my co-counsel and we met to write a brief for the Court of Appeals. He and I and a stenographer spent an entire day at the task and about four o'clock the stenographer left with a twenty-page, triple-spaced, hideously interlined, much corrected and recorrected "rough draft," such as no one but an experienced legal secretary can ever decipher. When she was gone, Calvert asked for a glass of water. He drew a pint of bourbon out of his briefcase, relaxed with sips of Kentucky's most famous product, and told me the following story.

After he relinquished his ample salary from Ford Motor Company, Calvert had cause to regret his decision. When he decided to enter general practice the coal mines were booming, and there were thousands of miners. The glow of prosperity warmed the land. There were innumerable cases for the lawyers–homicides spawned by Saturday night sprees, workmen's compensation claims for injured miners and the widows of the uncountable dead ones, and no end of Prohibition violations.

But the depression came early to the coalfields of southern Kentucky. Mines had multiplied past belief after 1910. By the mid-1920s there was a glut of the fuel in the southern and western states, and postwar economic troubles in Europe had shrunk the demand for export shipments. The boom ebbed away. The ranks of clients in the waiting rooms of lawyers were thinned, and many of those who continued to come were destitute. These unfortunates still needed lawyers as much as ever but could pay little or nothing for their services.

Conditions had gotten pretty tight at the Calvert home when Christmas approached in 1928. Legal fees had become discouragingly few and meager, and the pinch was felt at all levels. The house needed paint, and the Calvert family could have used some new clothes. Food was ample but tended to be inexpensive and ordinary. Payments were being met, but just barely, and the bank account was empty. Calvert viewed the future with apprehension.

Judge A. M. J. Cochran had scheduled a two-week session of the United States District Court to be held at London, Kentucky, beginning in mid-December. Hope springs even when the future appears most grim, so with a dubious heart Calvert resolved to attend the term. Perhaps some of the myriad defendants would have both money and the good sense to hire him as their attorney. Even a couple of hundred dollars would be immensely helpful. He would wager the certain expense of a hotel room against the uncertain possibility of fee-paying clients.

The little town of London was a drab place in those days. The farms that surrounded it were worn out and joined their poverty to the destitution of the highland coal fields that converged upon it. He found the federal courthouse jammed with a swarm of lanky, overalled men and goodly numbers of skinny, jaded women. Nearly all were charged with making or selling corn whiskey, or possessing it for the purpose of sale, or transporting the stuff, or sheltering other persons thus offending. Nearly all were guilty as charged but, with few exceptions, claimed to be innocent or offered heart-rending circumstances in extenuation. The most common pleas were poverty (being "up agin it, fer shore"), and having a large brood of children who would starve to death if either parent was locked up. They had profuse excuses, alibis, and justifications, but, alas, they had no money. One offered the counselor ten gallons of good whiskey–"made with water from the drip of the house and so good you can taste the malt real sweet and strong"–while another proffered a "right young milk cow and a suckin' calf" in return for his services, but none had cash.

After four days in which he collected little more than his expenses, Calvert returned to the courtroom on Friday morning. When court convened, the marshal brought in a slender youth whose wrists were handcuffed and fastened by a short chain to a broad leather belt that encircled his waist. Calvert was impressed by the young man's calm, self-assured bearing which was diminished by neither the heavy restraints nor the gazing of spectators. The young man was not more than twenty-two, about six feet tall, handsome and erect. His hair was brown and, though beginning to need a trim, was neatly combed. His features were striking and he glanced at Mr. Calvert with the bluest and frankest eyes the lawyer had ever encountered. Before the youth said a word Calvert was convinced that he was not guilty, that the government was absolutely wrong in the charge it had brought against him.

The indictment was read and Calvert's faith wavered somewhat. It appeared that a couple of weeks earlier federal agents had stopped a truck coming out of Tennessee through Cumberland Gap. It was loaded with whiskey, and the defendant was driving. The truck bore an Illinois license and no one else was in it. The indictment charged him with two counts: possessing an alcoholic beverage in violation of the Volstead

Act, and transporting same for the unlawful purpose of selling it.

When Judge Cochran asked him whether he was represented by an attorney, he answered that he was not. Asked (in those far-off pre-Miranda days) whether he was ready to plead to the charge, he said that he was. When the Court inquired whether his plea was "guilty" or "not guilty," Calvert leaned forward to observe his face and hear his answer. The defendant looked at the aged judge and in a clear, ringing voice replied, "Not guilty, Your Honor."

Coming in this straightforward manner, the declaration of innocence left His Honor quite obviously disconcerted. He looked at the defendant for a long moment, doubtless pondering the overwhelming character of the prosecution's evidence, but determined that the presumption of innocence would be fully protected. When he spoke again his tone had softened somewhat.

"You say," began the judge, "that you have no attorney at this time. That being so, do you have the financial capacity to retain an attorney to defend you in this case?"

The answer was as distinct as before. "No, Your Honor, I am sorry to say that I have no money."

Judge Cochran inquired whether he had relatives or friends who were interested in assisting him. Again the reply was negative.

It was the duty of the Court under these circumstances to enter an order designating an attorney to serve as the defendant's counsel. Under the law, the attorney would be required to work without pay. Every lawyer with appreciable trial experience had assumed such uncompensated duties dozens of times, and few ever grumbled at the burden such trials imposed upon them. (In the January 1949 term of Letcher Circuit Court—my first term as an attorney—I defended three alleged murderers under such court appointments.) Still, it would be an inconvenience for the lawyer who would doubtless have other things in mind for the day. To go to trial with court-appointed counsel was an indignity a defendant had to cope with throughout the proceedings, and suddenly this was an affront Calvert did not want this youth to bear. Then, too, Cleon K. Calvert had a combative, irrepressible nature and suddenly he felt the distinct need for a hard fought courtroom battle. Such a struggle would help him cast off his depression, and anyway, the boy said he was innocent and, by God, he might be telling the truth! He certainly looked like he was telling the truth.

Calvert had a son of his own, and who could tell what dark moments might lurk in his future? He might stand before a judge some day, innocent of the charge against him but doomed to suffer because he lacked money to employ a lawyer. Christmas was only a few days away, and red and blue lights had begun to gleam through wintry dusks. Carols were already being hummed by children who whispered about hoped-for gifts. A softer spirit was felt in the land, a sense of brotherliness and charity. It was a season of doing for other people. A good son of the Covenant, Calvert believed in the New Promise. Hard times had strapped him this year so that he could do little for his own wife and child, but he could do something for this unknown, friendless, chained, and penniless young man! He stood up, cleared his throat, and addressed the Court.

"May it please the Court, Your Honor! I understand that this defendant has no attorney and no funds with which to retain one. In order to save the Court the necessity of appointing a lawyer to defend him, I now offer to do so to the best of my ability and without any charge. This is, of course, contingent upon my services being acceptable to the defendant and conformable to the desires of the Court."

Calvert's eyes met those of the defendant for a long moment. He remained standing while Judge Cochran expressed the gratitude of the bench for this commendable proposal. The judge then explained to the youth that the gentleman who had just addressed the Court was Mr. Cleon K. Calvert, an experienced, able, and ethical lawyer. The Court suggested that his offer of free legal services be accepted and inquired whether the defendant had any objection to the arrangement. The reply was, " I have no objections at all, Your Honor, and I am grateful to Mr. Calvert for his kindness."

The Court again commended the attorney for his lofty action—an action, he said, that demonstrated a high regard for justice and its handmaid, the Law. The clerk entered a minute reflecting Mr. Calvert's offer, the defendant's acceptance, and the Court's approval. Thereupon court was recessed for an hour to allow counsel an opportunity to discuss the case with his new client and to make such other inquiries as he might think proper.

In the conference room the attorney again sized up his client from head to foot. He was impressed anew by the young man he had so impetuously undertaken to save from the federal penitentiary at Atlanta. As he phrased it to me thirty years later, "Innocence just oozed from that boy!" He learned the defendant's name from his own lips. From that source the good Irish cognomen sounded much less suspect than when read by the clerk and hedged about by the harsh, labored language of the indictment. After a few questions calculated to put his client at ease he asked him to start at the beginning and relate all the circumstances that had brought him to his present hard plight.

In quiet tones and without a single dubious flicker of an eyelash, the young man told his story. He was an orphan. His father had died ten years earlier when the defendant was twelve years old. There had been another child of two at the time, and his mother was pregnant. This situation left the mother with three infants, and in those days before Social Security and Public Assistance, she faced starvation. She moved her brood to a two-room, cold-water flat in one of Chicago's seediest districts. She worked as a seamstress from dawn to dusk but could earn only the scantiest subsistence. Her oldest son worked at such odd jobs as he could find, and his dimes and quarters went into the family till. At seventeen he left school to work full time, and for a year or two the family had a much easier life. Then the factory where he worked closed down and jobs became scarce. He went back to part-time and occasional employment, and his mother and brothers suffered real want. To make things worse, his mother became ill and had to spend much time in a charity hospital. This had caused him to assume almost total responsibility for the family. Then one day something totally unexpected happened. It was something that gave him real hope for a time.

He had been pounding the pavement in search of a job when he dropped in at McGinty's poolroom to escape from the biting autumn wind. He had no money for a game but watched others for a few moments before resuming his quest. As he started to leave, one of the other spectators touched him on the arm and asked whether he could have a few words with him. They went aside to a corner and there he heard a most unusual proposition.

The man was about forty, dressed in a sporty blue suit with an expensive white shirt and silk necktie. A diamond stickpin gleamed in the knot of the cravat. He had learned our hero's name from someone else in the poolroom, but did not identify himself. Names are unimportant, he said, in an honest transaction. And, on being expressly asked, he unequivocally declared the deal to be an honest one, "legal and aboveboard in every way."

This is what he wanted done. On the morning of the next day a van-type truck of a certain description would be parked in a nearby alley. His new and needy young friend would go there by 5 A.M. He would find the cab unlocked, the ignition key under the rubber floor mat. Enough money would be there to pay for gasoline and other expenses, and a road map marked with the routes to be followed. The truck would be driven southward across Indiana and Kentucky, through Cumberland Gap to the little town of La Follette in the hills of Tennessee. It would be parked across the street from the town's only hotel, with the keys left under the floor mat. The night would be spent at the hotel, and on the following morning, after a good breakfast in the hotel's dining room, the driver would return to the truck, retrieve the keys from precisely the same place, and, following the same route, would return the vehicle to the spot in the Chicago alley. He would leave the keys under the mat and go home. On the following day at noon he would return to the poolroom. There he would be handed $300.

It was all simple and easy, honest and lawful. He was being given the chance to earn the money because of those orphaned brothers and their ailing mother. The proposal ended with a friendly nudge in the ribs and, "Because it is getting close to Christmas, I wouldn't be surprised if there happens to be an extry fifty as a bonus."

The recipient of this unusual proposition hesitated. It was all very odd and yet, on the face of it, he would be doing nothing to break the law. He possessed a driver's license and had operated similar trucks. He could make the trip without difficulty. He could not be suspected of stealing the truck because he would return it to the same place. Still, it was dubious, no doubt about it. But there, again, were his sick mother and those two ragged brothers for whom Christmas held no promise. Three hundred dollars would pay old bills and buy new presents. "I will do it!" he said.

The next morning he was at the alley at precisely five o'clock. The truck was at the appointed place and all proceeded according to the plan and the carefully marked road map. He drove all day with only a couple of brief stops, traversing a bit of Illinois, most of the length of Indiana, the rolling Kentucky Bluegrass country, then the rugged hills north of Cumberland Gap. The truck was in excellent condition and slid through "the Gap" an hour after darkness had blanketed the wild ridges. At eleven o'clock the truck was cooling its engine opposite the little hotel, and he was a registered guest inside. He had traveled 650 miles and was numb with fatigue. A late snack was followed by nearly six hours of sleep—the peaceful sleep of the physically weary and spiritually restored.

Before dawn he was on his way north. This time, though, there was a difference. The padlock that held the rear doors was still securely in place, but the truck was no longer empty. While he had slept, someone had filled the van with a considerable cargo. It made no sound when he pulled the truck onto the empty street, but the weight was there, more than a ton of it. He could not see inside and he could not imagine what he was hauling. Consoled by the assurance that all was on the up-and-up, he pushed the gears into high and sped toward the historic gap he had read about in his grade school history books.

A mile inside the Kentucky border he rounded a curve to see a roadblock stretched across the highway. There were three cars and several armed men. One of them carried a submachine gun and two others held Winchester rifles. He braked the truck to a halt and his troubles began. The men were federal officers with a search warrant for his mysterious vehicle. A roadside search followed the breaking of the lock, and his astonished eyes beheld stacks of cardboard boxes. An agile agent jumped inside, tore open a carton, and lifted out a tightly sealed quart fruit jar. When the top was twisted off, he smelled for the first time in his life the pungent odor of southern moonshine whiskey. A count revealed that each carton contained a dozen jars, and there were forty cartons.

"I've been in jail ever since, Mr. Calvert. So far as knowing what was in the truck, I am as innocent as the judge." Then with a shrug, "But I guess no one will believe me if I swear it for a hundred years."

Calvert heard the tale with incredulity and astonishment. He wanted desperately to believe the prepossessing youth, and yet it was so preposterous, so fantastic. Would hard-eyed jurors ever swallow such a yarn? Probably not, but then Christmas was near and strange things happen at that gentle season. His fighting spirit flared. "Let's go tell it to the jury," he thundered.

The trial was brief, lasting only a few hours. A jury consisting of a couple of coal operators, a merchant from Harlan County, three or four miners, and a half-dozen hill farmers were interrogated, accepted by both prosecution and defense, and sworn by the clerk to "try the case and a true verdict render." The government called as its first witness an agent who described mammoth bootlegging operations in Chicago and told how the source of the whiskey had been traced patiently back to the Tennessee hills. An informant had telephoned to say that the truck had arrived, and he had worked all night to organize the roadblock and obtain the search warrant. Another agent told about the stopping of the truck, the breaking of the lock, the finding of nearly 500 quarts of whiskey. He handed up a jar of the stuff, took off the lid, and passed it around so the jurors could sniff it. Calvert noticed that one or two of them practically drooled as the forbidden liquid was handed back to the officer. The witness pointed his finger at the defendant and identified him as the driver of the truck and its sole occupant. The road map, marked with red ink along routes to be followed, was studied by the jurors. The prosecution rested its case and the triumphant district attorney looked at defense counsel with an air that said, "Come on, Calvert! Quit kidding yourself and give up. You can't squirm out of this one!"

Calvert disdained to make an opening statement and immediately beckoned his client to the witness stand. He did not disappoint his attorney. The manacles had been removed for the trial, and he stood as straight as a soldier, his hand raised at a right angle to take the oath required of a witness. His voice was clear and vibrant as he gave his name and background, and unfolded in careful detail the same story he had previously related to Calvert. While he talked, his bold blue eyes were on the jurors, looking at them in the easy way of unsullied truth. His manner was calm and dignified, without a trace of the flippant or smart-alecky. His voice sank when he told of his dying mother and little brothers who waited in expectation of Christmas. The same voice was strong, confident, and unyielding in response to a fiery cross-examination by the outraged attorney for the United States. On no single point did he yield ground. Instead he used the harsh interrogation to restate and reemphasize previous testimony, doing so at precisely the places where a bit of underscoring was helpful.

When his testimony ended and he stepped down, Calvert concluded that his client was the most masterful witness he had ever seen in a courtroom.

The judge then instructed the jury, laying a bit too much emphasis on the sanctity of the law, Calvert feared. He directed the attorneys to sum up and Calvert strode to a point in front of the jury box. His emotions were mixed, somewhat like those of a man who is about to be hanged and knows that he deserves it. That story, he gloomed, was weak as well water, but still, one never could tell with absolute certainty. More than one juror had gazed longingly at the prohibited fluid, and after all, it was only a few days to Christmas–and jurors might soften their hearts somewhat at this most pleasant of seasons. Besides, he was proud of his fighting Scotch-Irish ancestry and here he was, in a perfectly outlandish situation, working without any hope of remuneration, but in defense of a young man sprung from the same emerald sod. "If they convict, " he said to himself, "they'll beat two good men at the same time."

With the courage of a bantam rooster assailing a dozen game cocks, he drew himself to his full height and laid it on the line for the poor, wronged orphan boy from the wicked city.

He surmised that this was no time for fireworks and opened in a low and solemn voice. He knew several of the jurors personally and reminded them of the fact. He spoke of the grave duty of a lawyer in a criminal case, a duty to present the case fully and fairly that justice might be done. He reminded them of their own immense responsibility to weigh all the evidence, to put aside prejudice, not to be influenced or overawed by the immense panoply and power of the federal government. He mentioned their duty to a stranger who enters their midst, as this young defendant had done, and quoted a few appropriate words from Jesus on the subject. There followed some comments about widows and the sons who aid them in their ill health and destitution. "A son who honors his mother," he said, his voice rising almost to a shout, "is not a liar and a rogue! The undisputed evidence in this case shows that the defendant is in the dock today because he remembered and obeyed God's holy commandment to love and support the dying woman who gave him birth!"

Calvert paused to let that shaft sink home and perceived that all the jurors were listening with rapt attention and that some of them were positively glaring their disapproval at the nettled district attorney.

Calvert resumed. There were more references to parents—to the dead father, the dying mother—and to the two little brothers whom someone would have to feed and clothe. "There are no hands for that task except those that were brought before you this morning, chained like the hands of a slave though no jury had yet declared him guilty of anything! Chained notwithstanding the presumption of innocence! Chained like a condemned man headed for the gallows before ever a judge or jury heard a single word from his own lips!"

He talked of holy constitutional safeguards and over zealous law officers who trample them underfoot. At this, more jurors began to glare at the prosecutor and the agents who sat with him at his mahogany counsel table. Then Calvert took up the subject of wicked men who tempt the young and innocent into crime, destroying them for their own vile profit. Juries, he reminded them, must stand as a shield to make certain such malignant ruses do not succeed. Only juries could prevent the unscrupulous from ensnaring unknowing young men in diabolical plots calculated to ruin them, while the real malefactors stayed safely hidden to count their corrupt lucre. Such men have always existed, he murmured. "One of them was named Judas, and he betrayed Jesus Christ."

He reminded them that they were bound by an oath to try the case according to the evidence alone. The evidence stood uncontradicted. It was true that the truck was loaded with whiskey and the defendant was driving it. Likewise there was no dispute about how the accused came to be there. "This mighty government with all its money and men has not brought you a word of testimony from anybody that this boy has lied to you! The district attorney wants you to guess that he lied, and then send him to the penitentiary for it."

Calvert directed a few words at the Harlan County

merchant whom he suspected to be the strongest personality on the jury. Calvert knew that he had been orphaned in infancy, had grown up with his grandparents, and had lost his eldest son at Argonne Forest. He alluded to the sorrow and handicap of growing up without the counsel of a father to guide one in shunning evil influences. Young men just like this one had died by thousands on the gory fields of France to make the country safe for democracy. Democracy would be used to poor ends if that same kind of lad went to prison while the real wrongdoers walked the streets. In that event, those legions of fallen boys would have died in vain.

He ended with Christmas, then only a week away. "A special feeling is in the land at this time of year, a feeling that softens passions and makes people better," he said. "Our Saviour died to bring that spirit into the world for the benefit of all people everywhere. The quickest way to choke off the life of that widow in Chicago is to take away her boy. If Christmas morning finds her son in prison instead of by her side, he will never go back to her arms. When the prison doors open for him it will be too late to visit her bedside. He will visit her grave instead!"

On this histrionic note he sat down. The jury sat silent and unmoving. Obviously he had given them things to ponder and they were pondering them.

The district attorney shot to his feet as if rocket-propelled. He rushed to the lectern and opened with a voice that quavered with indignation. "Gentlemen of the jury, I have practiced law for a good many years, before numerous judges and hundreds of juries. I can say without a shadow of a doubt that the defendant's yarn in this case is the most fantastic cover-up for a crime I have ever heard, anywhere, anytime. And, in the same class with it, his counsel has begged you to turn him loose and let him go back to his wholesale bootlegging just because he says his mother is sick! My God, gentlemen, we don't know that he has a mother. She may have died years ago. She may have been the one who sent him on this outlandish journey in the first place. We do know, though, that he was arrested while driving along with nearly a hundred and fifty gallons of moonshine whiskey! The only connection this case has with the Christmas spirit was the stuff in those jars. It was intended for the Christmas trade in the Chicago speakeasies and, in my opinion, if the government agents hadn't caught him when they did, this defendant with his innocent-looking blue eyes would have been there behind the counter on Christmas Eve doling it out to the customers for two dollars a drink!"

There was considerably more in the same vein. Derision, ridicule, and venom was dumped on the defendant as the prosecutor retraced the trip from "that imaginary cold-water flat" to the poolroom, across two states to the "moonshine whiskey mills of Tennessee." He concluded with a wag of his finger under the defendant's nose, and, "He's innocent all right! Yes, indeed, he is. Just as innocent as Judas Iscariot was when he went out and hanged himself!"

The jury was out about forty minutes, and Calvert agonized in the torment of suspense known only to trial lawyers. His client was composed and calm. He spoke only once, to thank his attorney for trying so hard to save him. "Don't give up," Calvert admonished, "Uncle Sam has not won this case yet."

When the jury returned, the merchant–he of the orphaned boyhood and fallen son–was in the lead clutching the written verdict. A hush fell as the verdict was handed up to the judge, who read it and passed it over to the clerk. "Is this your verdict, gentlemen?" Judge Cochran asked. All murmured, "It is, Your Honor."

The clerk cleared his voice, adjusted his glasses, and read, "We, the jury, do agree and find the defendant not guilty on all counts of the indictment."

It was the end of the day, and the dejected revenue agents and the district attorney filed wearily from the room, frustration stamped in the sag of their shoulders. Calvert took his new friend, now free and visibly elated, aside for a final word. "You were lucky this time, son, but luck runs out. The next jury may put you in the jail and throw away the keys. Don't tempt fate, don't push your luck!"

The strong young hand came out to shake Calvert's in a firm, convincing grip. "Thanks for the advice as much as for all the rest you have done for me. This lesson was a hard one, but I will never forget it." The steadfast blue eyes gazed into Calvert's own. "An experience like this lasts a lifetime. All I want now is to get home and find a job. The straight and narrow is the road for me!" Then with a twinkle, "No more poolroom sessions of any kind."

Calvert pulled out his thin wallet and handed him a ten-dollar bill. "This will buy you some food along the way. I suppose you already know how to hobo and hitchhike."

"I'll make it," he replied, "and I will see that you get your money back. I'm down on my luck now, but someday I will have a job and wages. When that day comes you will be paid for what you did today. You will not lose a cent on this day's work."

Calvert left him in front of the courthouse. "Tell your mother and two little brothers that I send them a Christmas greeting in the words of Tiny Tim, 'God bless us every one!'" At the corner when he turned to look back through the gloom of the December dusk the youth still stood on the courthouse steps, the ten-dollar bill in his fingers, gazing after his benefactor. Each waved at the other in a final good-bye.

In the days that followed, Calvert's heart glowed with the warmth that comes only from good works. He had taken on a hard and thankless task, had prevailed against heavy odds, and had seen justice done. Doubtless his conduct had brought joy to a Chicago widow, but it had added nothing to his purse. When he returned to his own wife and tiny son, his prospects were as unpromising as before. So the days passed. The weather was unusually gray and cold. His boy–little Cleon, Jr.–had been prepared for the likelihood that Saint Nick would bring few gifts this year. All had accepted their straitened circumstances with good grace. Anyway, with the spring the economy would improve, fees would flow again, the bleak times would lift. Despite all that had happened, Lord Calvert was a hopeful man.

Christmas came on Tuesday that year. On Sunday he got up early and went to church. The sermon dealt with the gift of the Magi, and the carols included *Silent Night, Good King Wenceslas, Away in a Manger,* and *I Heard the Bells on Christmas Day.* Calvert enjoyed the musical program and, as it ended, congratulated himself that even those who were pinched for money could share in this, the best part of the yuletide. When the congregation had dispersed he went to his office and picked up the Courier-Journal an ambitious paper boy had left by his door. On the way home he stopped at the post office and checked his mailbox. He twirled the dial on the old-fashioned combination lock, and the little door swung outward on its hinges. He peered within. There was a single thin white envelope.

He opened the tiny letter knife at the end of his gold watch chain and slit the end of the envelope. There was no return address but the envelope bore a Chicago postmark. He drew out the contents and blinked in amazement. Then he realized that there really is a good Spirit of Christmas that comforts those who do justice and truly believe. What he held in his fingers was a long, slender check, printed on expensive blue paper and drawn on a Chicago bank. It read: "Pay to the Order of Cleon K. Calvert the sum of $2,500."

It was signed, "Al Capone."

Attached to the check by a paper clip was a crisp new ten-dollar bill.

Christmas

The glory and the pageantry will pass
Into another year's oblivion
Like August evening sounds in meadow grass.
Our offerings and songs will linger on.
The taste of winter in sharp winds is here,
Another year has come and sung its songs;
Too many people still are filled with fear,
Bewildered in this world of rights and wrongs.
God's spirit will be more than Christmas Day
When we find haven in His reverence;
We must live in His Spirit all the way,
To follow Him will make the difference.
All will have homes, warmth, food: all be befriended
When He comes first before festivities,
All fears on earth will be so nearly ended
With God's dimensions added to our lives.

Jesse Stuart

Deceᴍbeʀ Niɢhᴛs

He filled the room with loud imaginings.
Branches at the window, crooked and black
against the moon, turned reindeer antlers
clicking together, drawing Santa's shadow
along the wall. Out of the pages of books
camels strode, stately and aloof.
Wisemen jostled with elves all warted and wenned,
chattering and sawing, screeching and scurrying so
he thought surely his father would come to see
why elves hummed and hammered in the room,
why camels walked overhead. Then he would
wish the room a creche—so still the only
sounds were straw rustling, a lamb dreaming
in baa, the Christchild sucking his fist.

Jim Wayne Miller

There was a Silence

When He was born
I know
There was a silence
In the Christmas snow
Within the woods
Where squirrels slept
In hollow Beeches
Filled with mast
And last year's leaves.

Glistening, humbled Maples bent
Like bows
With feet, and heads,
and hands
Upon the ground.

From half-way around the world
He leapt from the virgin's womb

And
Mountains,
Already risen
And worn,
Paused . . .
Holding breaths
Like precious babes
And waited
For the world
To be transformed.

James B. Goode

The Old Guy With Whiskers

'Twas the night before Christmas when Maw up an' said.
"I've had it today," and headed fer bed.
I had on my long johns an' Maw wore her flannel
And she looked mighty cute in th' light from her candle.

The Young'uns was asleepin' as sound as a dollar
When a ruckus was raised in the pines 'cross the holler.
I saw through the' winder of our big settin' room
A sight for sore eyes in th' light o' the moon,

An old guy with whiskers was a-comin' our way
With a passel of reindeer a-pullin his sleigh.
Th' snow was piled high where th' wind had it drifted
An' it shimmered right purty, like jewels when it sifted.

Th' snow was a-swirlin' 'round driver and deer.
They came on like gangbusters, then took t' th' air.
"Get in there, you shitepokes," he called t' th' pack,
"Let's hustle it up if y' want t' get back!"

He whistled and shouted with all o' his might,
"You've got t' get crackin' or we'll be here all night,"
They swung 'round my pickup an' Maw's chicken coop,
Flew over the smokehouse an' lit on th' roof.

They slid t' a stop by th' tall chimley stack
An' he clumb down th' chimley with a pack on his back.
He looked kinda raunchy with ashes and soot
All over his whiskers an' britches an' coat.

But he paid no attention t' th' smudges of black
An' he got down t' business by openin' his sack.
"Ho, Ho, Ho!," his belly laugh rolled out like thunder
As he crammed every stockin' with all kinds of plunder.

"Set a spell an' I'll fix y' some good home-cooked grub,"
Maw offered him kindly when he finished his job.
He was powerful hungry an' allowed he was able
T' eat all the vittles Maw put on th' table.

He et all th' fixins then said t' Maw "Maybe
I could go fer some seconds on biscuits and gravy!"
He was took with Maw's cookin' but he jest couldn't stay
So it was back up th' chimley t' his deer an' his sleigh.

He jumped in the sleigh and th' reindeer lit out.
"Come back now, y' hear?" I called with a shout.
Then I follered as Maw led th' way with the candle.
She was shore mighty cute in her gown of red flannel.

Marlin W. Blaine

Return of the Old Guy With Whiskers

On th' night before Christmas I was plum' tuckered out
But Maw hummed a tune as she hustled about.
She'd fed all th' young'uns an' put 'em t' bed
An' was rollin' some dough fer a pan o' hot bread.

She was shore mighty fetchin' in her flannels of red
An her gown matched th' nightcap she wore on her head.
I ast her what fer she was cookin' a bite.
She said, "We're a-lookin' fer th' old guy t' night!

It's pert nigh a year since that feller was here–
The old guy with whiskers a-drivin' th' deer."
Then I dozed off a spell from a-bein' so tard
An' fell off my rocker when somethin' thumped hard

Up thar on th' roof by th' tall chimley stack
Then th' old guy drapped in with th' sack on his back.
His big "Ho-Ho-Ho" made a jolly good noise
As he crammed all th' stockins' with trinkets an' toys.

Maw ast him was he hungry an' he said, "I shore am!
I was hopin' you'd have some good eatin' on hand.
I'm a-feelin' right hungry an' 'pon my pore soul
I ain't had no vittles since leavin' th' pole!"

"I'll set out some grub that'll stick t' yer ribs.
Some biscuits an' gravy an' fresh gingerbread."
He et ever' smidgin o' th' vittles Maw set,
Pushed back from th' table an' took a deep breath.

He picked up a fancy wrapped package an' then
Retch over t' give it t' Maw with a grin.
"I brung y' a present fer a-makin' my day!"
Then he clumb up th' chimley t' his deer an' his sleigh.

I hurried outside fer t' tell 'em good-by
An' I waved as they headed up into th' sky.
He called t' th' deer an' they circled about,
Then I heerd his big laugh as they picked up their route.

When I come in th' house Maw was flouncin' around
In a new frilly cap an' a red silk nightgown!
She danced through th' house as we headed fer bed
An' was shore mighty cute in that outfit of red.

Th' old guy with whiskers had done it agin–
Makin' Christmas right happy fer me an' my kin.
It was plain t' be seen th' old geezer was smart–
He knowed how t' git t' mine and Maw's heart.

Marlin W. Blaine

About the Authors

Jesse Stuart (1906-1984) was a famous Kentucky writer and teacher. He published more than 2000 poems, 460 short stories, and more than sixty books, which have immortalized the Kentucky hill country that inspired his writing.

Billy C. Clark, "the chronicler of the Big Sandy region," writes about the unique river culture of southern Appalachia. Today this native of Catlettsburg, Kentucky lives in Farmville, Virginia and edits *Virginia Writing,* an award-winning publication which features the writing and art of high school students.

Thomas D. Clark is Kentucky's Historian Laureate. He has authored numerous books and articles and is the moving force behind the new Kentucky History Center. He is one of Kentucky's best known and most admired citizens.

James B. Goode, a creative writer, journalist, and film maker was born in Benham, Kentucky, a company coal town built by International Harvester. Today he is Professor of English at Lexington Community College.

Loyal Jones, now retired from his long-time position as Director of the Appalachian Center at Berea College, is a published expert on Appalachian music, religion, values, and humor.

Jim Wayne Miller (1936-1996) was one of the brightest and best-loved speakers and writers in southern Appalachia. A native of western North Carolina and a Vanderbilt University Ph.D., Miller taught at Western Kentucky University until his death.

Harry M. Caudill (1922-1990) A lawyer, author, college professor, and recipient of the Purple Heart during World War II, Caudill was a nationally respected authority on the problems of Appalachia. His book *Night Comes to the Cumberlands* brought national attention and assistance to Appalachia's distress.

Marlin W. Blaine, a retired employee of Ashland Inc., is a native of a rural area of West Virginia near Point Pleasant. He and his wife Lucille proudly claim six children and eight grandchildren.